# WING COMMANDER CONFEDERATION HANDBOOK

Incan Monkey God Studios
Chris McCubbin, Chief Archivist
Austin, Texas, TERRA
1998.271

# SECURITY CHECK

## LOGON

Loading BIOS.......no errors detected......analyzing port information.....OP port connection data cartridge device........IP port connection networked port id110983095893............. hub 8979w8734 socket 876786 .......initializing voice input mode.......

please enter ID

>>2309879-9m707

## CHIP INITIALIZATION

Initializing chip reader slot ....... Please insert security chip .... Analyzing ........ Chip accepted ..... Valid passcode entry can clear you to ...... Top Secret level. Please enter command.

>>read data chip

Reconfiguring chip reader slot ..... Insert data chip .... Analyzing ..... Chip accepted ... Analyzing .......

Chip access limited by logon ID .... Recall logon ID=2309879-9m707 ..... Searching access files ..... ID matches file, chip contents follow

Chip contains 24 files + subfiles. All files result of data search. All classified files protected by security codes. Command code required to view files. Confidential, Secret and Top Secret files not available to this user ID for download or hard copy transfer.

## LEGAL

### HarperEntertainment

*A Division of HarperCollinsPublishers*
10 East 53rd Street, New York, NY 10022-5299

ISBN 0-06-107553-1

HarperCollins®, 📖®, and HarperEntertainment® are trademarks of HarperCollinsPublishers Inc.

First printing: March 1999

Printed in the United States of America

Visit HarperEntertainment on the World Wide Web at http://www.harpercollins.com

10 9 8 7 6 5 4 3 2 1

A record of your user ID and data session will be permanently appended to this data chip. Continue?

\>>yes

#  DATA DISK CONTENTS

## WELCOME/CREDITS

Welcome to CDATANET, network system of the Confederation Armed Forces. Network creation and maintenance by Incan Monkey God Studios |
Lead Writer=Chris McCubbin | Additional Writing=Melissa Tyler | Graphic Design=Sharon Freilich, Jennifer Spohrer | Additional Design, Advertisement Design/Management=Tuesday Frase | Editor=David Ladyman.

Incan Monkey God Studios wishes to thank=Lawrence Freilich, scientific illustrator | Etienne Braun of Black Box Photo (Luxembourg, TERRA) for personnel photos | NASA and NSSDC=suppliers of photos and data | Chris Roberts and Origin Systems for creating the Wing Commander Universe | Digital Anvil, especially Jason Schugardt, Ashley Galaway, Eric Strauss, Chris Brown, Marten Davies | Rand Marlis, Creative Licensing Corp. | Sterling Belefant, Alan Smithee Films | HarperCollins: John Douglas, Rich Miller, Dianne Walber, Jeannette Jacobs | Peter Telep, historian

IP Port Status: undocked     OP Port Status: undocked
Clearance Key Status: insertcard_verifying_denied_accepted
Data Security Level: unclassified_confidential_secret_topsecret

View   Store   Delete

## ADMIRAL TOLWYN: EXCLUSIVE INTERVIEW
There's a certain feeling of awe, the first time you step into Admiral Geoffrey Tolwyn's quarters . . .

View   Store   Delete

## History of the Terran-Kilrathi War
The Terran Confederation and the Kilrathi Empire first came into contact on 2638.229 . . .

View   Store   Delete

## History of the Pilgrim War
The first major interstellar military conflict, the Pilgrim War was fought . . .

View   Store   Delete

## WAR HERO KILLED IN ACTION
Space Force Major Arnold Blair was killed in action over Peron yesterday . . .

View  Store  Delete

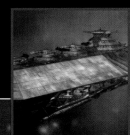

## Excerpt: Joan's Ships of Known Space

**The following data files are the property of Joan's Interactive Data, Ltd. . . .**

View  Store  Delete

## SF Lt. Cmdr. Kien Chen's Death

**Please allow me to express my deepest sympathy on the death of your husband . . .**

View  Store  Delete

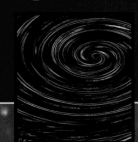

## Every Citizen's Guide to Practical Science

**There are three basic types of modern starship drives. *Impulse drive* is the standard . . .**

query "news update" media=popmag, level=UNCLASSIFIED | return=7
Retrieving 7 text files + graphical subfiles . . . Keying search #315AZ.
Please insert data chip . . . You may view, store, or delete.

article 1 of 7="admiral tolwyn"
article 2 of 7="terran-kilrathi war, history"
article 3 of 7="pilgrim war, history"
article 4 of 7="death, sf maj arnold blair"
article 5 of 7="joan's ships of known space"
article 6 of 7="death, sf lt cmdr kien chen"
article 7 of 7="jump physics, layman"

**UNCLASSIFIED**

# In Step With . . .

# Admiral Tolwyn

*In a Jubilee exclusive,*
*Davis Davis interviews the architect of*
*the Confed War Effort*

**By Davis Davis, Jubilee Senior Editor**

There's a certain feeling of awe, the first time you step into Admiral Geoffrey Tolwyn's quarters in the Titan military complex. It's not just the fact of being in the presence of one of the three most important men in the Confed war effort—it's a feeling that comes from the rooms themselves. The admiral's personal quarters are pleasant, modest, scrupulously clean and orderly . . . and curiously sterile. Entering them carries something of the air of entering a pyramid or descending a lunar crater—going somewhere where human feet haven't been for a very long time.

"Home" is not a concept that means much to Confed's Chief of Fleet Operations these days. Or, if anything, "home" is a cabin on the *Concordia*, the admiral's flagship.

Today, however, the *Concordia* is several sectors away (exact location deeply classified, of course), continuing its ongoing operation in support of the border defenses, while the admiral has been recalled to Sol for a few weeks, to brief the Joint Chiefs and the Senate on the state of the war. Between the hotel room he occupied on Terra and the berth on the long-range shuttle that will return him to the front, he has a few days to catch up with affairs on Titan Base, and air out his Spartan home-of-record.

The Admiral is not a tall man—slender and compact, he seems designed by evolution for the narrow corridors and low hatches of a warship. His speech combines the cool, clipped efficiency of a captain at the helm, with the calm erudition of a college professor—both occupations that he has held in the past. Today he has put away the multitude of medals on the dress uniform that he wore while addressing Confed's leaders a day or two previous, and instead wears the simple fatigues of a deck officer. However, even in his informal guise his creases fall perfectly and his deck boots gleam.

When questioned about his unlived-in living quarters, the response is thoughtful. "I really do love it here on Titan. Not just being close to Earth, and Callisto and Mars, but the base itself. I like to feel it alive all around me. And I suppose I could do much of my job from right here, if I chose to. But I almost feel guilty, every time I come home like this. There are 40 million spacemen, marines and soldiers out on the frontier right now. Most of them have far more to come home to than I do, and most of them won't see their home again until this is over—if, indeed, they ever return at all. When they're all home again, perhaps then I can relax."

It's difficult to imagine a relaxed Geoffrey Tolwyn. The son of a wealthy and politically influential family (go back only three generations and you'll find four admirals, one general and three senators on the Tolwyn family tree), the admiral has relaxed very little in the almost four decades since he entered the Academy. Graduating first in his class, he went on to collect a masters in engineering and a doctorate in hyperphysics in record time. He earned his first star before his fortieth birthday, as an engineer building the first Grand Fleet in the Pilgrim war. A few months later, he gave up the star to take command of his first battleship, as part of the second Grand Fleet.

He did enjoy a few years between the wars, teaching physics at the Solar University in Reykjavík. But after the *Iason* incident, he was one of the first officers reactivated, part of the elite military brain-trust charged with seeing that Confed stood ready to go to war with an alien enemy. When war came he was quickly elevated to chief of Naval operations of the beleaguered Vega sector. Rising to his current post in the command upheavals of '46, he is officially the third most senior officer in the Confed Navy. In practical terms, however, he remains the primary strategic architect of the Confederation war effort—the one single man whose decisions most effect the odds of victory or defeat on a daily basis.

> "When they're all home again, perhaps then I can relax."

Finally seated in the admiral's quarters, this reporter begins with the question that Tolwyn has returned to Sol to answer, "How goes the war?" Not surprisingly, the answer is a precise summation of that given when the Senate asked the same question. "In not more than three years—and probably far sooner than later—we have every reason to expect the Kilrathi to launch on human space an attack of unprecedented scale. This invasion will be, by far, the greatest, most deadly conflict in the history of the human race. At the moment, our forces stand ready to meet this assault. The colonies at the front are, each and every one, an impregnable fortress, and our fleets are ready to fly on a moment's notice to meet any alien threat, large or small. However, our preparedness must not be taken for granted. The smallest slip in vigilance or in the quality of our support will be seen and ruthlessly exploited by the enemy."

Before the calm intensity of the admiral's eyes, the reporter almost fears to ask the next question. However, it's one that's on the tongue of every armchair strategist from the

> "We have already taught the cats respect. I fully intend to teach them fear as well."

metroplexes of Terra to the dust-farms of McClean, and the reporter performs his duty for the public. "Why the defensive posture? Why the long wait? Isn't there some way to take the battle to the cats?"

*CS Concordia in all her magnificence. Over 850 meters long, the Concordia is home not only to Admiral Tolwyn, but to over 1000 men and women of the Terran armed forces.*

The answer is calm but resolute. "Rest assured, we are not sitting idle behind our defenses. We'll have some unpleasant surprises for the Empire when they come, and if they don't come we'll have some even more unpleasant surprises to deliver to them. Nor must it be imagined that our long siege has been in vain. Kilrathi losses over the last decade have been astronomical. At least eight times our own, and possibly as much as twice that. The Kilrathi do not fear death, but you may believe that the Empire has felt the losses we have inflicted upon it. It is my opinion that if we can break the next Kilrathi invasion, it will be physically impossible for the Empire to mount another for decades, and that it will then be ripe for pacification, by force if necessary." Something hard and cold enters his eyes. "We have already taught the cats respect. I fully intend to teach them fear as well."

One more popular supposition needs to be answered. "What about the systems at the front? Many of them are still active civilian colonies. When the Kilrathi invasion comes, will they be abandoned like the frontier colonies in the early days of the Pilgrim war?" This question does draw a more impassioned response.

"Never! I was there when we retook those worlds, and I saw what was left. We will not abandon a single . . ." Suddenly the warrior remembers that he is also a politician. He takes a deep breath and chooses his words with care. "I don't wish to give the impression that I am criticizing the men who created the strategy of the last war. I understand why they had to do what they did. I'm just grateful that I didn't have to make their choice."

"Nonetheless," he continues, the fire rekindling in his face, "humanity now faces a far crueler foe than even the most fanatical Pilgrim. Retreat is not an option. I will never willingly surrender a single civilian colony to the Kilrathi. If we stand firm, the enemy will break himself upon the wall of our shields. If one fortress falls, the Emperor will find another equally strong beyond it. There will be losses, and I fear they will be terrible, but there will be . . . can be . . . no retreat. Humanity will stand, or we will die—those are the only options which our enemy has given us. I am here to see that we do stand, not just today and tomorrow, but forever. And never thief, nor tyrant, nor petty alien god shall ever cast us down!"

**M14TCN5 Portable Data Reader Unit**

Welcome to the *Current Events Annual* archives—"the chronicles and abstracts of our time."

If you are new to these archives and require assistance, request HELP.

Otherwise, list your keywords to begin searching.

>>kilrathi war, history

Thank you. Searching . . . Your request matched 1 article exactly:

# History of the Terran-Kilrathi War

The Terran Confederation and the Kilrathi Empire first came into contact on 2638.229, and conflict ensued immediately. On 2641.009, Confed formally declared war. From that day to the present, conflict has continued unabated, and the Kilrathi have uniformly refused any offers of cease-fire, truce or negotiation. At present, neither side possesses any clear-cut strategic advantage, and there are no signs of any abatement of aggression.

VIEW ARTICLE

REF KILRATHI/KILRATHI EMPIRE/TERRAN CONFEDERATION

>>ref kilrathi

Thank you. Referencing KILRATHI . . .

DISCOVER THE POWER
● PERSONAL ■ V.8.1
HOLOGRAPHIC UPGRADE
ASSISTANT AVAILABLE
by METADYNAMIX

LINK POWER REVISE

M-10X8.1

| SEARCH | PREV | NEXT | RELOAD | SAVE | PRINT | QUIT |

SCREEN 2 | query="terran-kilrathi war, history" | source=Student's
Encyclopedia Current Events Annual, 2653, HarperCollins, TERRA

## Kilrathi

The Kilrathi are a race of sentient, space-faring non-humanoid bipeds. They represent the first space-faring, non-human civilization encountered by humanity. The first recorded contact with the Kilrathi was made on 2638.229, when the exploratory vessel CS *Iason* encountered three armed Kilrathi merchantmen. Upon being haled by the *Iason*, the Kilrathi vessels opened fire and destroyed that ship. From that time to the present, a state of uninterrupted hostility has existed between Confed and the Kilrathi Empire.

The Kilrathi rule an Empire of unknown size, probably consisting of 300 to 500 inhabited systems. Kilrathi space abuts Vega and Gemini sectors, while Epsilon sector is roughly divided between systems colonized by humanity and those originally settled by the Kilrathi.

The Kilrathi are believed to have evolved from carnivorous pack-hunters, resulting in their belligerent and expansionistic territoriality. Kilrah, the capital of their Empire, is believed to also be the birthplace of the race. The Kilrathi Emperor is the hereditary leader of whichever noble clan is currently in power. The power of a sitting Emperor is legally absolute; however the Emperor's power or policies may be challenged by another clan, an action leading to vendetta. Such conflicts usually take the form of all-out civil war, with the throne staying with or going to the winner. Inter-clan challenge is also a common route of imperial succession. The current Emperor is believed to have taken the throne in 2632—a remarkably long contiguous reign without civil warfare. It is probable that the ongoing military aggression against the Confederation has served to stabilize the clans behind the current ruler.

NEXT SCREEN

**Kilrathi banners.** *These banners indicate clan lineage or affiliation— all members of the crew of a Kilrathi space vessel belong to the same clan, with officers chosen from the families of clan leaders. The vessel would then belong to that clan, and a united force is achieved only when the clans unite to fight a common enemy.*

**M14TCN5 Portable Data Reader Unit**

# Kilrathi (cont.)

There is evidence to suggest that Kilrathi star travel technology did not originate with the Kilrathi themselves, but may have been acquired from some other, unknown race. The question of the origin of Kilrathi technology must ultimately remain open until such time as humanity gains access to the Kilrathi's own historical record.

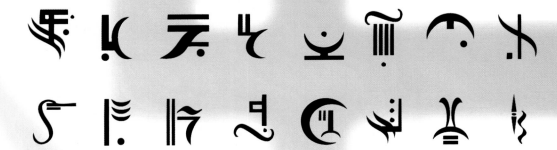

**Sampling of the Kilrathi alphabet.** *The Kilrathi language is for the most part ideographic—each symbol representing a word or idea, as do the characters of the Chinese language. However, in this language, the dots and small squares in each ideograph appear to act as modifiers that alter the meaning of the main symbol—they have been observed to appear in different places and combinations around the main graph.*

*Terran cryptologists and linguists continue to decode and study captured transmissions in an attempt to uncover the secrets of this mysterious calligraphy.*

BACK TO HISTORY OF TERRAN-KILRATHI WAR

REF KILRAH/KILRATHI: POLITICS/KILRATHI: PSYCHOLOGY
KILRATHI: SOCIETY/KILRATHI: TECHNOLOGY

>>back to history

Thank you. Loading HISTORY OF TERRAN-KILRATHI WAR . . .

SCREEN 4 | query="terran-kilrathi war, history" | source=Student's Encyclopedia Current Events Annual, 2653, HarperCollins, TERRA

# History of the Terran-Kilrathi War

Following the *Iason* incident, Confed interdicted all non-military exploratory, trade and colonization activity beyond the Vega sector frontier. At the same time they began a coordinated covert scouting operation to determine the extent of Kilrathi dominion. By the end of '38, Confed analysts had determined that the Kilrathi sphere of influence was at least equal to, and possibly greater than, that of humanity. Four separate envoys (under heavy escort) were sent into Kilrathi space in an attempt to at least open up lines of communication, but all such efforts were met by armed aggression. (All four missions were able to retreat under fire back to Confed space.)

At the same time, the Kilrathi were probing Confed defenses. There is evidence of covert scouting analogous to Confed operations, but most of the contacts in this period consisted of pirate attacks on Confed shipping. A significant breakthrough occurred on 2638.348, when a CSF patrol at Masa surprised a Kilrathi corvette in the act of looting a free trader. Because most of the Kilrathi crew was aboard the Confed vessel when the patrol attacked, the corvette was taken with only minimal damage. Although the Kilrathi privateers were all killed in the fighting, the corvette provided a wealth of important intelligence, including the best data yet on the total radius of Kilrathi space, inhabited Kilrathi colonies near Confed space, and multiple new jump-routes within Kilrathi space.

The conflict escalated on 2639.006, when a Kilrathi carrier group attacked and destroyed the agricultural colony on Hellespont, an unarmed settlement of assimilated Pilgrims. 82,000 humans were either killed or enslaved in that attack. About 12 hours later, a similar force attacked the shipping port of Tartarus, but that colony was able to hold out until reinforcements arrived from Brimstone Naval Station, and the Kilrathi withdrew after 48 hours of heavy fighting. On 2639.007—less than eight hours after news of the attacks reached Terra—the Confederation Senate passed a formal declaration of war against Kilrah.

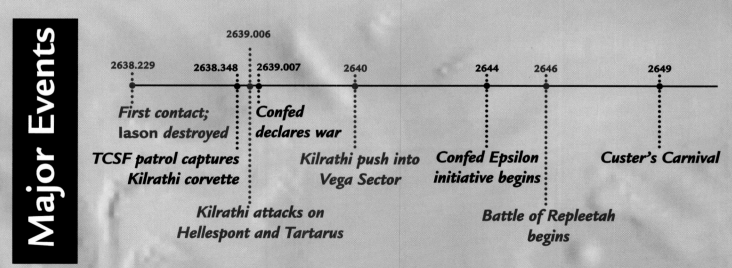

**Major Events**

| 2638.229 | 2638.348 | 2639.006 / 2639.007 | 2640 | 2644 | 2646 | 2649 |
| --- | --- | --- | --- | --- | --- | --- |
| First contact; Iason *destroyed* | TCSF patrol captures Kilrathi corvette | *Confed* declares war / Kilrathi attacks on Hellespont and Tartarus | Kilrathi push into Vega Sector | Confed Epsilon initiative begins / Battle of Repleetah begins | | Custer's Carnival |

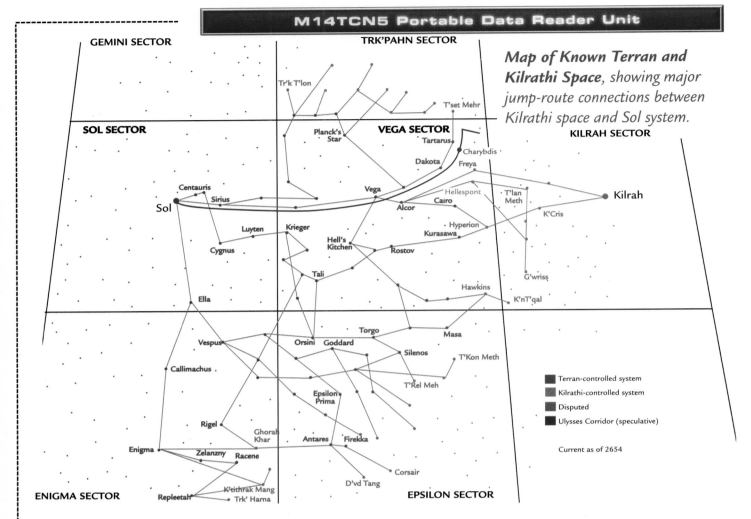

**M14TCN5 Portable Data Reader Unit**

*Map of Known Terran and Kilrathi Space*, showing major jump-route connections between Kilrathi space and Sol system.

Terran-controlled system
Kilrathi-controlled system
Disputed
Ulysses Corridor (speculative)

Current as of 2654

The escalation of hostilities did not catch Confed totally by surprise, and within a week they were able to launch a punitive counter-offensive centered on the K'nT'qal system. Kilrathi defenses held, but the action provided time to fully implement wartime defenses on all border colonies, using ships originally built for the two Grand Fleets of the Pilgrim war.

In the decade and more that has passed since the beginning of the Kilrathi war, the battle lines have shifted remarkably little. Between 2640.160 and .200, the Kilrathi launched a major assault that resulted in a temporary Confed withdrawal from about 30% of our systems in Vega, but a Confed counter-offensive retook nearly all the lost colonies, between 2640.220 and .340. In late 2644 the Kilrathi repulsed a Confed attempt to bring all of Epsilon sector under its control. T'Kon Meth and T'Rel Meh fell after heavy fighting, but the invasion effort stalled there. A Kilrathi counter-offensive in 2646 took both worlds back, and led directly to the Battle of Repleetah, the longest (2646.080 - 2651.290) and bloodiest battle of the war. When the Kilrathi finally withdrew from Repleetah, it was estimated that Confed had lost more than 2.7 million troops (in addition to 1.2 million civilians lost in the early phases of the battle), while Kilrathi losses are estimated at upwards of 7 million.

SCREEN 6 | query="terran-kilrathi war, history" | source=Student's Encyclopedia Current Events Annual, 2653, HarperCollins, TERRA

In '49 the Terrans launched the last major offensive in the war to date, an all-out assault on G'wriss. Terran ground troops established a beachhead, but stronger-than-expected space defenses wiped out most of the invasion's space support. An emergency relief group was launched to evacuate the ground forces and bring them back to Confed space. The carrier CS *Tiger Claw* spearheaded the relief operation, fighting a grueling three-day delaying action which resulted in the death of more than half her fighter pilots. This action has become known in popular reports as "Custer's Carnival."

Since Custer's Carnival, Confed's strategy has been one of all-out defense—to allow the more aggressive Kilrathi to hurl themselves into battle at a disadvantage. Kilrathi casualties have been astronomical; however, to date the Empire appears undeterred. Confed analysts speculate that more-or-less continual warfare is a long-established bedrock of the Kilrathi society and economy, and that the Kilrathi are not expending a catastrophically larger percentage of warriors in the ongoing war with Confed than they would have lost in inter-clan warfare in an equivalent time frame. In the last few years of the conflict, however, Kilrathi aggressive attacks have declined precipitously, but with no corresponding decline in defenses or increased willingness to negotiate.

*Famous artist Mariano Diaz's rendering of a Kilrathi General in full armor.*

Confed strategists have warned that it is probable that the Emperor has succeeded in unifying the clans to the point where he can withdraw and amass forces for an invasion effort of unprecedented scale. In the face of this foreboding likelihood, Confed is left with little choice but to double and re-double their defenses along the border, and hope that when the hammer finally descends, it will break on the stone.

**M14TCN5 Portable Data Reader Unit**

# History of the Pilgrim War

*(Excerpts from The Student's Encyclopedia, 123rd Edition, HarperCollins, Bonn, TERRA, 2653)*

The first major interstellar military conflict, the Pilgrim War was fought between forces of the Terran Confederation and the colonial Pilgrim Alliance from 2631 to 2635, beginning with the Battle of Titan and ending with the fall of Peron. The Pilgrim Alliance surrendered unconditionally on 2629.334, after which all Alliance worlds were absorbed into the Terran Confederation.

## VIEW ARTICLE

### REF PILGRIM ALLIANCE/TERRAN CONFEDERATION/BATTLE OF TITAN
### SIEGE OF PERON

>> ref pilgrim alliance

Thank you. Referencing PILGRIM ALLIANCE . . .

## The Pilgrim Alliance

The Pilgrim Alliance was the first organized effort by humanity to colonize other solar systems. Between 2311 and 2588 they colonized 12 systems in Sol and Vega sectors, using hopper-drive "sloships." Radical religious separatists, the Pilgrims believed that they were the "elect" of human-ity, with the exclusive divine right to live outside the Sol system. In 2635 a Pilgrim fleet attacked the Terran Confederation Port of Titan starbase in an attempt to cripple Confed colonization efforts. Over the next four years the resulting conflict brought about the end of the Alliance. In 2635 the Pilgrim Alliance was formally dissolved, and all extant Pilgrim worlds were brought into the Confederation as protectorate colonies.

*Background Graphic: Pilgrim Cross*
*The Pilgrim dagger-cross is the most sacred symbol of the sect. The dagger represents divine judgement against unbelievers, and the cross symbolizes the salvation of the elect.*

*Pilgrim crosses worn as jewelry (like the highly ornate one pictured here) traditionally keep the sharpened dagger blade feature. For safety's sake, the blade can be sheathed, or recessed into the cross with a spring-trigger release. Some of the more ornate crosses are believed to have been chemically treated so that they glow or shimmer in response to the wearer's body chemistry.*

SEARCH | PREV | NEXT | RELOAD | SAVE | PRINT | QUIT

SCREEN 2 | query="pilgrim war, history" | source=Student's Encyclopedia
urrent Events Annual, 2653, HarperCollins, TERRA

# History

e historical roots of the Pilgrim Alliance lie in the solar expan-
on of the 22nd century and the ecocatastrophe of the 23rd. In
67 the United Nations established Olympia Station, the first
rmanent human settlement on another planet. Supported by
ace stations on Phobos and Luna, the Olympia colony
came the primary staging area for humanity's migration to
e outer planets of the Sol system. By 2215 the U.N. had estab-
ned further permanent colonies on the moons of Jupiter and
turn, placed research facilities on the satellites of Uranus and
ptune, and landed on Pluto. In that same timespan Terra
came ever-increasingly reliant on the outer planets for heavy
dustrial metals.

*Mars was the site of Olympia Station, the first Terran settlement on another planet.*

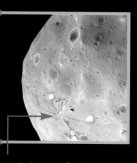

*Mining colonies—such as this early one on Mar's inner moon, Phobos—supported the plane-tary bases as humanity expanded outward.*

*Eventually, such colonies would allow the outer planets the self-sufficiency they needed to maintain the quarantine of Terra.*

In 2219 the first of the Great Pandemics
appeared. After the loss of Luna
Station, the outer planets sealed themselves off entirely from earth. ˉ
rules were simple—for the duration of the medical emergency, no ˙
from Terra could travel beyond the Legrange transit stations. Any colo
who chose to return to Terra could not return to space until such tim
the quarantine was lifted.

It was possible for the outer planets to seal themselves off, because
this time the colonies were virtually self-sustaining. Oxygen and wa
could be obtained from the rings of Saturn and the ice caps of the la
outer moons, while mineral resources were prolific on Mars and
asteroid belt, with the resources of the outer moons held in reserve. M
exotic compounds were being siphoned from the outer atmosphere:
Jupiter and Saturn.

Terra, struggling against the ever-rising tide of disease and fam
became increasingly reliant on the mineral wealth of the outer planet:
sustain the remnants of its faltering production infrastructure. With
sil fuels virtually exhausted and the biosphere turning ever more hos
Terra became completely dependent on the outer planets for fuel and
raw materials for self-contained hydroponic systems that provi
Terra's only safe food supply.

These imports were dropped impersonally down Terra's gravity well, with no physical contac
between Terra and her colonies. At first, Terra could trade data and cultural resources for thes
raw materials. However, the colonies became more self-sufficient and their indigenous cultur
continued to evolve, while Terra's data and cultural industries fell prey to the general economi
and social chaos. The colonies were faced with an ever-increasing demand from Terra, bu
ever-diminishing expectations for fair payment. Meanwhile, on Terra, popular resentment wa
growing against the rich, healthy, and aloof extraterrestrials.

## The Final Exodus

The emergent culture of the outer planets was ripe for new and radical philosophies. The mos
successful of these new worldviews arose from the writings of Ivar Chu McDanie
(2257–2311?), an organic chemist and lay-preacher assigned to the Neptune research base.

While stationed on Neptune, in 2294, McDaniel began to experience ecstatic visions. H
believed that in these visions he experienced direct communion with the Divine, receivir
prophetic revelations. He wrote of his experiences to friends on Mars, who encouraged him t
collect and publish his insights.

McDaniel claimed that he had been chosen to receive his visions because he was a spiritual
receptive individual located at the very fringe of human settlement of Sol system. McDani
taught that the prophesied apocalypse had occurred, but divine judgment was confined t
Terra itself. Those humans who had migrated to other worlds constituted an "Elect," destine
for physical and spiritual salvation and protection. However, because of the pervasive corru
tion of Terra, the divine presence could not fully empower the Elect as long as they remained
the Sol system. To complete their salvation, the Elect must undertake the "Final Exodus," lea
ing Sol system entirely to seek spiritual and genetic perfection among the stars. In McDaniel
mystical cosmography, Terra was Hell, the universe at large was Heaven, and the remainder
Sol system constituted a sort of Limbo where the chosen remnant could prepare itself.

McDaniel's views gained momentum in 2304, with the discovery of the Morvan Drive (popu
larly known as the "hopper" drive), which allowed interstellar distances to be covered in a ma
ter of months or years, rather than generations. By 2309 the Outer Planets Policy Council wa
firmly in the control of the McDanielites. In 2311 the first Morvan Colony ship was launche
Bound for the Sirius system, it contained 1200 colonists, including Ivar Chu McDaniel. Th
ship never arrived at its destination—orthodox pilgrim theology teaches that McDaniel and h
crew were translated directly to a higher plane of existence, from which McDaniel continues t
spiritually direct his followers.

**SCREEN 4 | query="pilgrim war, history" | source=Student's Encyclopedia Current Events Annual, 2653, HarperCollins, TERRA**

Subsequent sloship efforts were successful, however, to a degree that modern historians find frankly amazing. Missions to Alpha and Proxima Centauri, Cygnus and a second Sirius mission all arrived at their destinations and successfully established self-sustaining settlements. By 2350 regular trade routes were being established between Titan and the Centauri colonies. It was during this time that the McDanielists began to refer to those who took passage on the colony ships as "Pilgrims."

As the interstellar colonies grew, Sol system continued to send out new sloships. It was the sacred duty of all McDanielists to emigrate, and only devout Pilgrims were permitted to participate in the exploration and colonization program. By the end of the 24th century the Exodus was complete—all McDanielists had abandoned the Sol system. The effort depleted the Sol system colonies—outer planet populations in 2400 were less than a quarter of what they'd been a century before. Occasionally a semicovert trading mission from Sirius or Alpha Centauri would arrive at Mars or Titan, but little news would be exchanged.

Some time before 2450, the administrative center of the Pilgrim Alliance was established on Beacon, with the spiritual authority headquartered on McDaniel's World. From there, the Pilgrims began to push into the Vega sector.

### Map of the Sol Sector

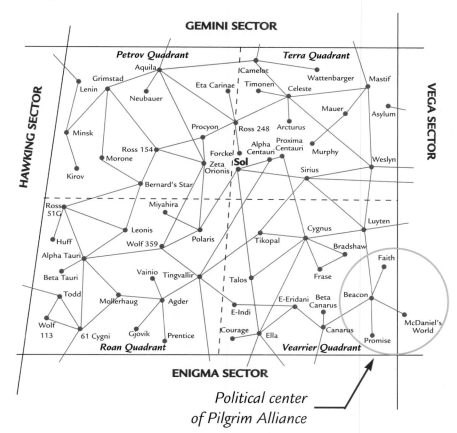

*Political center of Pilgrim Alliance*

**M14TCN5 Portable Data Reader Unit**

Meanwhile, back on Terra, the ecocatastrophe had finally played itself out, and humanity began to reestablish its social order. In 2423 the quarantine of Earth was formally lifted and Earth began to once more interact with the rest of the Sol system. While the mineral resources of the outer planets were absolutely essential to the rebuilding of the Terrestrial industrial base, throughout most of the 25th century Solar humanity had little leisure to devote to exploration or pure research.

Nonetheless, the Pilgrims noted with some alarm that Terrestrials were once more venturing beyond the orbit of their own moon. In 2462 a heavily armed Pilgrim sloship entered orbit around Luna, demanding a meeting with Terra's leaders. The result of the following summit was the Treaty of Luna, which established Pilgrim title to all habitable worlds within 50 years sloship travel of Terra. Terra agreed to forsake all sloship exploration of other systems, and the Pilgrims agreed to a policy of strict non-interference with Sol system affairs. A few, strictly limited trade agreements were also arrived at.

(It is believed that sometime around 2500 the Pilgrims discovered the propulsion system that would come to be known as the Akwende, or "jump" drive. However, this development was kept secret from Terra.)

So matters stood for more than a century, until Terra's discovery of the Akwende Drive in 2588. A new breed of humanity began to reach out beyond its own star. Losses of exploratory missions were high—far higher than for the early Pilgrim expeditions—but 26th-century Terra had the wealth and population to easily absorb the losses. Terrestrial explorations respected Pilgrim space, but jump routes were soon established that reached beyond the Pilgrim sphere. Sol began to establish colonies of its own, leaving Vega sector to the Pilgrims but expanding out towards Hawking and Gemini sectors. The Pilgrim alliance vigorously protested this expansion as a violation of the Treaty of Luna, but the newly christened Terran Confederation took the stance that the Luna accords only prohibited sloship colonization and direct encroachment on Pilgrim space, neither of which described Confed's current policy.

In 2615 a militant faction seized political and religious control of the Pilgrim Alliance. To this day, most Confed citizens remain bewildered by the intense Pilgrim hostility towards Terra. It must be understood that, to Pilgrims, Terrestrial humanity was divinely cursed by definition (in fact, although the leadership knew better, many Pilgrim colonists had been led to believe that humanity was completely extinct in the Sol system). That anyone other than the Elect (Pilgrims) should venture beyond the orbit of Pluto was at best blasphemous and at worst diabolic. On a more pragmatic note, the Pilgrim leadership was suddenly faced with having to share a galaxy which they had hitherto regarded as their personal domain.

SEARCH  PREV  NEXT  RELOAD  SAVE PRINT QUIT

SCREEN 6 | query="pilgrim war, history" | source=Student's Encyclopedia
Current Events Annual, 2653, HarperCollins, TERRA

# The Pilgrim War

The Pilgrim leadership decided to cut off Terrestrial incursion at the source. At the time, all jump-capable ships were being built and launched from the Port of Titan space station. The Pilgrims assembled a jump-capable battle fleet and mounted a massive assault on the Port of Titan.

Evidence suggests that the Pilgrims expected to destroy Titan in a quick, surgical assault, then move on to a major show of force against Earth itself before returning to Beacon. On 2631.244, the fleet jumped into the Sol system. The Pilgrims planned for a overwhelming assault on a primitive and unprepared foe.

Instead, the Pilgrims discovered Confed to be strong, rich and ready for trouble. After three days of intense fighting around Saturn, the Pilgrims were repulsed with the Port of Titan station still intact. Believing they had proven their point, Confed offered a renewed round of negotiations with the Alliance. This offer was ignored.

The Pilgrims began an aggressive guerrilla action into Confed space, attacking colony worlds and disrupting shipping. On 2632.017, Pilgrim forces destroyed the Confed military outpost at Celeste, along with a mining colony on that world. One day later, Confed formally declared war against the Alliance.

*After three days of intense fighting around Saturn, the Pilgrims were repulsed with the Port of Titan station still intact.*

Confed adopted a defensive posture and mobilized its industrial resources into a full war footing, while the Alliance, encouraged by early successes, continued its offensive against the more remote colonies. Confed colonials on worlds occupied by Pilgrim forces were placed under harsh and oppressive conditions. Mass executions were common, and millions were pressed into slave labor. While colonies still under Confed control were aggressively defended, little effort was expended to liberate occupied worlds. This was misinterpreted by Pilgrim leaders as a sign of weakness.

Instead, Confed was concentrating its resources on assembling a massive invasion force in the Sol system. Confed strategy was to not be drawn into an expensive and drawn-out hit-and-run battle with the Alliance, but instead to mount a coordinated invasion targeted on the center of Pilgrim power. On 2633.235, the Grand Fleet was launched. Over the course of the next five months Centauri, Sirius, Cygnus, Frase, and Bradshaw fell in rapid succession. Faced with mounting expenses and devastating losses, the increasingly desperate Pilgrims staked everything on an all-or-nothing defense of the agricultural colony of Peron, in the Luyten system. The siege of Peron held for seven months, while each side mounted increasingly brutal sorties and counter-offensives, each trying to find some crack in the other's defenses.

**M14TCN5 Portable Data Reader Unit**

In the end, it was the Confed industrial machine and the resource wealth of the Sol system that carried the day. On 2634.288 the remnants of the Confed Grand Fleet were reinforced by a new strike force almost half again the size of the original. Peron's defenders were overwhelmed in two weeks of brutal fighting, and when the Confed joint fleets jumped into Beacon system on 2634.359, they were met with an offer of surrender. The Pilgrims offered to immediately stand down their military and dissolve the Alliance government in return for guarantees of the safety of Pilgrim civilians, and certain limited rights to autonomy for non-military Pilgrim worlds, particularly McDaniel, the spiritual center of the Pilgrim religion. After six weeks of negotiation, peace accords were signed at Cygnus on 2635.049, at which time the Pilgrim Alliance officially ceased to exist.

## Post-War Pilgrim Remnants

Since the treaty, many former Pilgrims have been re-integrated into Confed society, either as individuals or on a system-wide basis. At this writing, three systems and five colonial enclaves remain semi-autonomous, with severely limited contact with the rest of the Confederation (although they remain subject to CSF observation and inspection against renewed military activity). Shortly after the surrender, the order went out from McDaniel that all remaining Pilgrims were to refrain from any space travel, as a collective penance for the war—or, more specifically, for losing the war. Consequently, all practicing Pilgrims have applied for conscientious objector status in the Kilrathi conflict, and all Pilgrim colonies remain officially neutral. So far, even the loss of two Pilgrim systems to Kilrathi aggression, and ongoing Kilrathi incursions into former Pilgrim space, have done nothing to shake the order's neutrality.

**>>load file seige of peron/blair**

Searching . . . Loading DEATH, SF MAJ ARNOLD BLAIR . . .

SCREEN 1 | query "death, sf maj arnold blair" media=obit,
level=UNCLASSIFIED | source=Solar Newswire Service, 2634.302

# WAR HERO KILLED IN ACTION

## PERON

Space Force Major Arnold Blair was killed in action over Peron yesterday, according to casualty lists from the Grand Fleet Information Office. One of the architects of the Confed Grand Fleet, Blair was also a highly decorated fighter pilot.

Born on Terra in 2597, Blair studied cybernetics, earning a BA from the University of Kingston and a Masters and Ph.D. from the Sorbonne. In 2620 he was awarded the Golden Moebius for software design. After graduation, Blair signed on as a troubleshooter for Sung Datasystems, working on many colonies in Enigma and Argent sectors, and earned two letters of commendation from Confed Colonial Services. It was also during this time that he received his light space-craft pilot certification.

> Commodore Tolwyn released the following statement upon the death of Major Blair. "Arnold Blair was the true model of an officer, gentleman and scholar. We celebrate his heroic and honorable life, and grieve for the loss of a heart so pure and a mind so brilliant at such an early age. On behalf of myself and all the other officers who had the privilege of working with Major Blair, I wish to extend my profound sympathies to his family."

When Confed declared war, the Space Force activated Blair's reserve commission, and ordered him to report to Titan. He served a 25-month tour as a pilot aboard the carrier CS *Harrison*. During his combat tour he was certified a double-ace, with 11 confirmed fighter kills and two cap-ship kills, earning two Blazes for Conspicuous Gallantry.

In early 2633, Commodore Tolwyn picked him to join the (at that time deeply secret) Grand Fleet design team, where he was appointed senior cyberneticist. He was recently awarded a Conroy Medal and a Senatorial Commendation for his work designing software controlling Grand Fleet maneuvers.

In mid-year Blair returned to combat duty on board the CS *Foster*, earning three more confirmed kills and a citation for bravery.

According to the GFIO release, Blair was killed at about 0900 Terran Standard Time on .301, while flying alone in a Merlin-class fighter just above the atmosphere of Peron. It is believed that his craft was detected and destroyed by a Pilgrim automated stratospheric defense drone. The exact nature of Blair's mission is classified by Grand Fleet Ops.

Blair's wife, Devi, also died recently. He is survived by a son, Christopher, his mother, Melissa, and a sister, Jennifer, who is caring for Christopher.

The following data files are the property of Joan's Interactive Data, Ltd. Every attempt has been made to insure the accuracy of the statistics and text, and where information is dubious, this has been noted.

**CONFEDERATION FIGHTER**

# CF-117b Rapier

Currently the primary utility fighter of the Confed space force, development on the Rapier began in 2527 and the first order of 700 was commissioned in 2536. The B model, with enhanced missile capacity and the more efficient rotary-barrel neutron gun, was phased in beginning in '45, and the A model has been completely phased out. The Rapier has now largely supplanted the earlier CF-105 Scimitar, particularly in frontline operations. The Rapier combines acceleration, maneuverability and firepower to make it the premier one-on-one dog-fighter in space today. Its handling superiority is necessary, since its short-range neutron guns require close approach to the enemy in combat.

The Rapier's most distinguishing visual feature is its rotary-barrel neutron gun. The rotating multibarrel allows longer continuous neutron fire. The duel neutron pulse generators can be set to alternate or synchronous fire. Wing-mounted lasers provide longer-range fire support. It also mounts up to ten guided or dumbfire missiles.

The Rapier features the standard Confed Tempest targeting and navigational AI, and a jump-capable drive array. Its life-support systems are rated for up to seven hours cruise time. (A LARP variant exists, the 117b-L, with an enhanced sensor package and rated for up to 72 hours life support, but lacking the neutron gun.) The Rapier is not capable of sustained atmospheric operations—its wings function strictly as weapon/missile mounts. It can generate a retrieval tractor rated for up to 75 tonnes. It is capable of ejecting its pilot into a standard survival pod.

|  |  |
|---:|:---|
| *Class* | Medium Fighter |
| *Length* | 9 meters |
| *Mass* | 9 tonnes |
| *Cruise Velocity* | 250 kps |
| *Max Velocity* | 450 kps |
| *Weapons* | Two Wing-Mounted Laser Cannon |
|  | Duel-Pulse Rotary Barrel Neutron Gun (forward) |
|  | 10 Missile Mounts |
| *Armor* | Fore and aft phase shields rated to 7 cm |
|  | 5 cm fore armor/4 cm aft armor |
|  | 3 cm port/starboard armor |

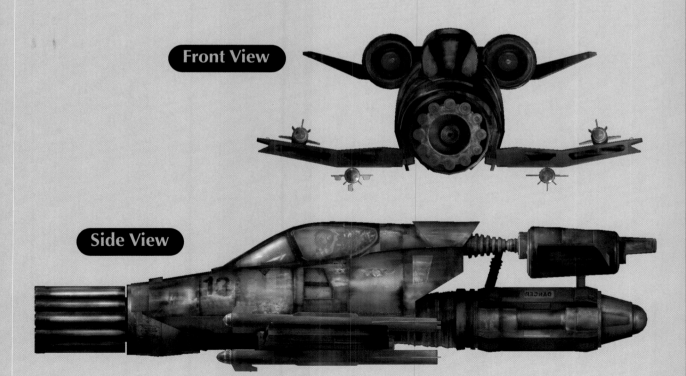

Front View

Side View

CONFEDERATION FIGHTER

25

## CONFEDERATION FIGHTER

# CF-131 Broadsword

The first Broadswords were deployed during the Pilgrim War to support Confed's invasion fleet. It still remains Confed's primary fighter/bomber. In 2648 all in-service Broadswords were upgraded to mount two antimatter torpedoes, but other than that change and minor upgrades to ship's systems, the Broadsword of today remains remarkably similar to those that flew with the Grand Fleet.

The Broadsword stacks an amazing amount of destructive potential into a compact package, but only at the expense of maneuverability. The Broadsword has virtually no evasive capacity— it has to either destroy attackers outright or rely on escorts of lighter fighters. On the plus side, its three recessed turrets can provide a full 360 degrees of fire support, and be set for independent or synchronized targeting. There's also a defensive AI mode that will automatically fire the turrets at any enemy targets of opportunity.

Like all Confed fighters, the Broadsword mounts a Tempest targeting and navigational system, and its drive array is jump-capable. The Broadsword is rated for up to 16 hours of life support. It can generate a retrieval tractor rated up to 150 tonnes. It is capable of ejecting the pilot in a standard survival pod.

Top View

| | |
|---:|:---|
| *Class* | **Fighter/Bomber** |
| *Length* | **12 meters** |
| *Mass* | **14 tonnes** |
| *Cruise Velocity* | **150 kps** |
| *Max Velocity* | **320 kps** |
| *Weapons* | **3 Mass-Driver Cannon (2 wing-mounted, one nose-mounted)** |
| | **3 Missile Mounts** |
| | **2 Torpedoes** |
| *Turrets* | **3; 2 Neutron Guns in each** |
| *Armor* | **Fore and aft phase shields rated to 13 cm** |
| | **10 cm each fore/aft armor** |
| | **8 cm each port/starboard armor** |

**CONFEDERATION FIGHTER**

Back View

**M14TCN5 Portable Data Reader Unit**

**KILRATHI FIGHTER**

# KF-100 Dralthi

There is anecdotal evidence that the Dralthi was the primary space fighter of all Kilrathi clans for as much as a century before first contact with humanity. Dralthi have been in the forefront of virtually every naval engagement of the present war. The utility fighter-ship of the Kilrathi arsenal, the lightly armed and armored Dralthi relies on its remarkable speed and maneuverability, plus effective group tactics, against superior Confed fighters like the Rapier.

From captured Dralthi, we know that the ship's targeting systems are at least equal to the best Confed can offer, allowing Kilrathi pilots to take the best advantage of the ship's limited offensive potential. Their life-support systems are capable of supporting a Kilrathi for about 10 hours (about four hours longer than an equivalent system could support a human, since Kilrathi physiology is better adapted to privation than a human's). Its impulse engines are based on the same basic concepts of ram-scoop technology used by the interplanetary craft of humanity.

Dralthi are not jump-capable. They can generate a light tractor beam rated to about 5 tonnes, used primarily for salvage. Dralthi do not have an ejection system—Kilrathi warriors are expected to live or die along with their fighters.

SCREEN 6 | subquery="dralthi" | sort=bestmatch | return=all
source=joanships.mil.fgtr.kil.083952

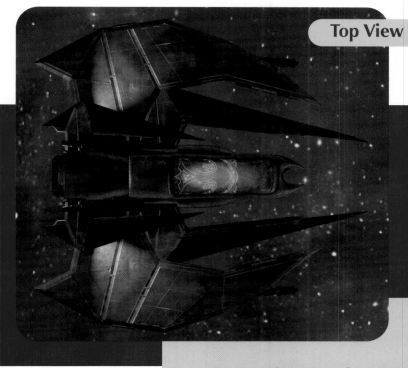

Top View

**KILRATHI FIGHTER**

| | |
|---|---|
| *Class* | Medium Fighter |
| *Length* | 9 meters |
| *Mass* | 10 tonnes |
| *Cruise Velocity* | 230 kps |
| *Max Velocity* | 400 kps |
| *Weapons* | 2 Laser Cannon (wing-mounted) |
| | 4 Missile Mounts |
| *Armor* | Fore and aft phase shields rated to 5 cm |
| | 4.5 cm fore armor/3.5 cm aft armor |
| | 3 cm each port/starboard armor |

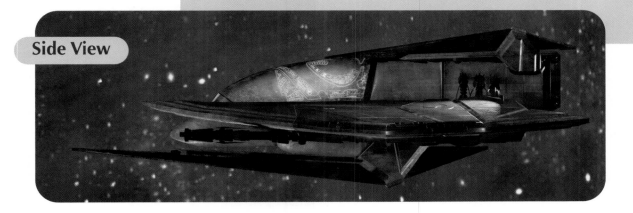

Side View

**M14TCN5 Portable Data Reader Unit**

**KILRATHI FIGHTER**

# KF-227 Salthi

This small, dangerously fast and maneuverable ship was seen more frequently in the early stages of the Terran/Kilrathi war. At present, it seems to be falling out of favor in the Empire, at least for front-line use. Intelligence suggests that the Salthi is still seeing a great deal of use deeper inside the Empire, for scouting and planetary defense.

A coordinated wing of four or more Salthi can represent a severe challenge to an opposing pilot, but their light defenses mean that even a single hit from most Confed fighters can take one out of action. Offensively, the Salthi's inability to respond to a missile assault with equivalent power is a debilitating flaw.

Salthi possess sophisticated targeting routines equivalent to those of a Dralthi. They are not jump-capable, do not mount a tractor beam, and have no ejection system. A Salthi's life-support system is capable of supporting a Kilrathi warrior for about 7 hours.

| | |
|---:|:---|
| **Class** | Light Fighter |
| **Length** | 6.5 meters |
| **Mass** | 12 tonnes |
| **Cruise Velocity** | 300 kps |
| **Max Velocity** | 480 kps |
| **Weapons** | 2 Laser Cannon |
| | 1 Missile Mount |
| **Armor** | Fore and aft phase shields rated to 3.5 cm |
| | 3 cm fore armor/2 cm aft armor |
| | 1.5 cm port/starboard armor |

# KF-402 Krant

The Krant seems to have predated the current conflict, but Intelligence believes that it was relatively little used, until it proved useful against Confed cap ships.

The Krant is more heavily defended, but much less maneuverable, than the Dralthi. It appears to have been originally designed for cap-ship defense. When the development of meson shielding made capital ships effectively immune to conventional ship-to-ship missiles, the Kilrathi pressed the Krant into service as a dive-bomber, capable of delivering a pair of antimatter torpedoes to a meson-shielded target. In that capacity the Krant has become (along with long-range strategic missiles) the Kilrathi's primary anti-cap-ship asset, a function which has currently nearly displaced their original purpose.

When configured for defensive operations the Krant deploys with four missiles and no torpedoes; when attacking an enemy cap ship it mounts torpedoes but no missiles. Krant bombers are virtually unique among Kilrathi pilots, in that they do not dogfight an enemy—they deliver their load to their target, and immediately return to their carrier to reload. (If possible. The Kilrathi have also been known to send Krant through jump points with one-use jump drives on suicide missions against Confed targets.)

Under normal mission conditions Krant are not jump-capable. They possess the same targeting and tractor systems as the Dralthi. Their life-support systems are capable of supporting a Kilrathi for about 15 hours. Like all Kilrathi ships, they possess no ejection system.

**KILRATHI FIGHTER**

|  |  |
|---:|:---|
| **Class** | Medium Fighter/Bomber |
| **Length** | 11 meters |
| **Mass** | 11 tonnes |
| **Cruise Velocity** | 200 kps |
| **Max Velocity** | 360 kps |
| **Weapons** | 2 Laser Cannon (wing-mounted) |
|  | 4 Missile *or* 2 Torpedo Mounts |
| **Armor** | Fore and aft phase shields rated to 6 cm |
|  | 6 cm fore/6 cm aft armor |
|  | 5 cm each port/starboard armor |

**CONFEDERATION CAPTIAL SHIP**

# Concordia–Class Supercruiser

Currently the largest battleship in Confed's fleet, the Concordia class was originally developed during the Pilgrim War. The original Concordia was named the Confed flagship in 2645 and serves as a mobile command center for Naval operations.

Defended by 30 point-defense missiles (for fighter defense) and 4 primary antimatter guns, the main offensive asset of the Concordia class is its 50 torpedo tubes, capable of launching both ship-to-ship and ship-to-planet munitions, including strategic weapons. It also mounts a small fighter deck capable of carrying a light squadron of about 20 medium fighters or fighter/bombers.

In keeping with its fleet command function, the Concordia class mounts enhanced long-range communications and sensor packages.

Standard protocol calls for a Concordia-class ship to travel in company with at least two destroyers and a cruiser (or larger battleship). Transports frequently convoy with a Concordia-class ship, since its fleet command function makes it a natural focus for ship tenders and other resupply operations.

The Concordia class takes 700 officers and crew, plus additional space for up to 350 working supercargo (command support and fleet operations personnel, plus a full hospital facility with a standing staff of 75). There's additional space for up to 300 hospital patients and up to 60 prisoners in the brig, plus limited accommodations for non-crew passengers.

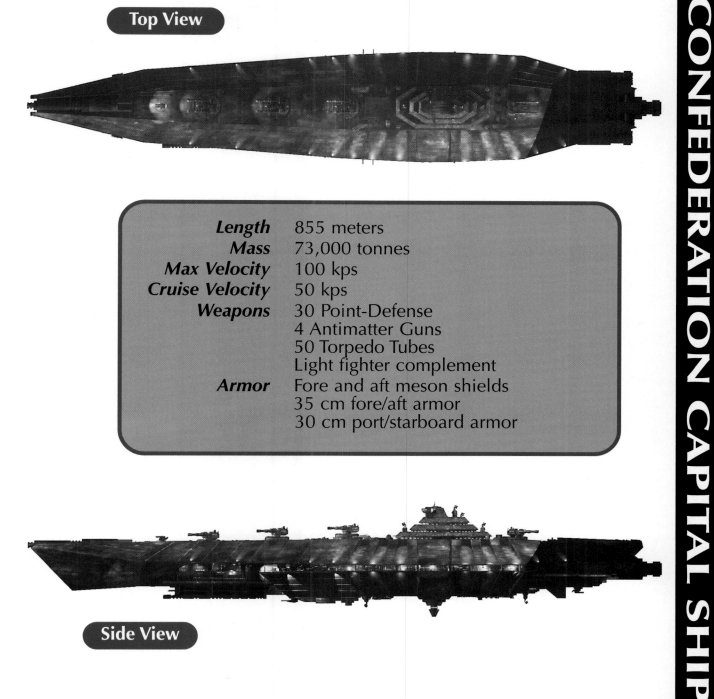

**Top View**

| | |
|---:|:---|
| *Length* | 855 meters |
| *Mass* | 73,000 tonnes |
| *Max Velocity* | 100 kps |
| *Cruise Velocity* | 50 kps |
| *Weapons* | 30 Point-Defense |
| | 4 Antimatter Guns |
| | 50 Torpedo Tubes |
| | Light fighter complement |
| *Armor* | Fore and aft meson shields |
| | 35 cm fore/aft armor |
| | 30 cm port/starboard armor |

**Side View**

CONFEDERATION CAPITAL SHIP

33

CONFEDERATION CAPITAL SHIP

# Bengal–Class Strike Carrier

The Bengal class has been Confed's primary utility carrier since before the Pilgrim War (first commissioned in 2619). Development on a replacement carrier is ongoing, with a scheduled rollout no later than 2657, but for now the sturdy Bengal remains the mainstay of Confed's fighter operations.

The Bengal class includes hangar space for up to 104 fighters or bombers— enough for one to four full squadrons (depending on the ship's mission). Given reasonably experienced pilots and crew, a Bengal is capable of executing a full flush scramble (launching all 104 fighters) in as little as 12 minutes.

Modern Bengal-class ships carry enhanced map room imaging facilities for planning tactical operations. Crew capacity is 550 (including pilots and flight deck personnel), plus space for a marine complement of 50. In addition to full hangar and repair facilities for its fighters, a Bengal class can also carry and service corvettes and light transports with a cross-section of no more than 35 meters.

In addition to its fighter complement, the Bengal class mounts eight turreted lasers for antifighter defense. Its torpedo tubes are primarily used for ship-to-ship munitions, but can be modified for strategic ship-to-planet devices.

Rear View

Top View

| | |
|---|---|
| Length | 625 meters |
| Mass | 55,000 tonnes |
| Cruise Velocity | 70 kps |
| Max Velocity | 130 kps |
| Weapons | 22 Point-Defense |
| | 8 Turreted Lasers |
| | 40 Torpedo Tubes |
| | Fighter complement |
| Armor | Fore and aft meson shields |
| | 24 cm fore/20 cm aft armor |
| | 25 cm port/starboard armor |

CONFEDERATION CAPITAL SHIP

KILRATHI CAPITAL SHIP

# Snakeir–Class Super-Dreadnought

The largest warship in the known Kilrathi arsenal, the Snakeir was first observed in battle in late 2649. It is believed to carry hangar capacity for at least 200 fighter craft. In addition to serving as a large carrier, its other purpose is to act as a space-to-planet missile platform, launching high-orbital and even interplanetary munitions on static targets. Recently, reports of long-range, self-guided ship-killer torpedoes being launched from Snakeirs at Confed warships have filtered through.

The capacity and capabilities of the Snakeir are highly speculative, as an intact specimen has never been taken in combat. Extrapolating from known design specs of earlier Kilrathi warships, it probably has a complement of officers and crew between 400 and 600 strong, plus additional space for up to 500 warriors, trained to serve both as pilots and as marines.

A Snakeir is usually accompanied by at least three destroyers or cruisers, with at least a dozen Krant escort fighters guarding the force at all times. It is often found escorting Kilrathi transports to the front.

51 individual Snakeirs have been reported engaged in operations on the front, of which four are known to have been destroyed in battle, and two believed lost to accident or mishap. All known Snakeirs have borne the markings of the imperial house, suggesting that the individual clans and worlds of the Empire do not sponsor Snakeir production, but that the Emperor has personally commissioned these ships for use in the Confed conflict.

SEARCH  PREV  NEXT  RELOAD  SAVE  PRINT  QUIT

| | |
|---|---|
| *Length* | **915 meters** |
| *Mass* | **67,000 tonnes** |
| *Cruise Velocity* | **100 kps** |
| *Max Velocity* | **150 kps** |
| *Weapons* | **42 Point-Defense** |
| | **6 Turreted Lasers** |
| | **14 Torpedo Tubes** |
| | **Fighter Complement** |
| *Armor* | **Fore and aft meson shields** |
| | **28 cm fore/24 cm aft armor** |
| | **36 cm port and starboard armor** |

**Top View**

Remember—you saw it here first. Joan's was the first civilian information organization to carry reports of the Snakeir. As soon as Joan's learned of the discovery of this vessel, we had our data analysts combing transmissions for the statistical information you see above.

**Joan's Ships of Known Space**
*Information you can count on.*

KILRATHI CAPITAL SHIP

37

M14TCN5 Portable Data Reader Unit

KILRATHI CAPITAL SHIP

# Sivar-Class Dreadnought

The Sivar class is believed to predate the Terran/Kilrathi conflict. It is the premier main battle ship in the Kilrathi fleet, and a Sivar can be found at the heart of almost all Kilrathi task forces. More than 700 distinct Sivar-class vessels have been identified in action. It is the closest thing the Kilrathi have to a carrier in the Confed sense of the term, and carries hangar space for up to 150 fighters. Its missile capacity, by contrast, is rather limited, and is confined mostly to ship-to-ship torpedoes.

The Sivar class has exceptionally powerful impulse engines, making it the fastest large battleship currently in space. This speed, combined with its copious and efficient carrier capacity, provides its major strategic asset; the Sivar class can move quickly into position, launch a fighter strike on its objective, then move rapidly to a new assignment.

The Sivar class is believed to require a crew of 300, plus an additional 300 warriors for fighter and marine operations. The configuration and capacity of the Sivar class is quite well known, due to the fact that several have been captured largely intact over the years (most notably, an unarmed but otherwise completely functional ship taken in dry-dock early in the Epsilon initiative). Sivar-class warships have been observed with the markings of all the major noble clans, but increasingly they're being disproportionately seen with imperial clan markings, indicating the ongoing centralization of strategic forces under the Emperor himself.

Side View

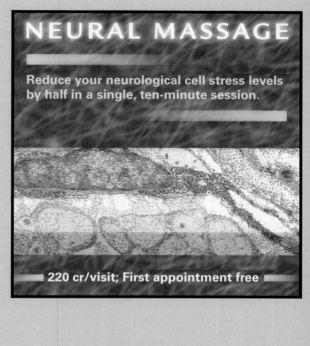
**Top View**

**KILRATHI CAPITAL SHIP**

| | |
|---:|:---|
| *Length* | 825 meters |
| *Mass* | 61,000 tonnes |
| *Cruise Velocity* | 100 kps |
| *Max Velocity* | 200 kps |
| *Weapons* | 23 Point-Defense |
| | 6 Turreted Lasers |
| | 12 Torpedo Tubes |
| | Fighter Complement |
| *Armor* | Fore and aft meson shields |
| | 28 cm fore/18 cm aft armor |
| | 26 cm port/starboard armor |

**M14TCN5 Portable Data Reader Unit**

KILRATHI CAPITAL SHIP

# Thrakhra–Class ConCom

The newest addition to the Kilrathi fleet—it was first reliably reported in 2652—the Thrakhra class appears to represent a significant shift in Kilrathi strategic planning. The Thrakhra class is apparently a ship designed for the express purpose of fleet command and communications, with deliberately limited offensive capacity.

Only seven Thrakhra-class vessels have been authoritatively identified in action, and none has yet been destroyed or taken by Confed, so information about these ships is extremely tentative at this time.

Based on known crew complements of similar-sized vessels (the Fralthi-class cruiser), the Thrakhra class probably carries about 200 officers and crew. Confed intelligence theorizes that it also carries a very small contingent of warriors (probably 50 or less), but a large contingent of fleet support specialists, including strategists, intelligence analysts, and communications and sensor techs.

The Thrakhra class mounts only two laser turrets, and its fighter deck seems to be extremely small—probably including hangar capacity for around 12 ships, just enough to provide limited escort capacity. It does seem to carry a significant missile loadout, however, particularly of the ship-to-planet variety. It is theorized that this allows the Thrakhra class to complete cleanup operations after an objective is taken, freeing main battleships to take up defensive positions or pursue fleeing ships.

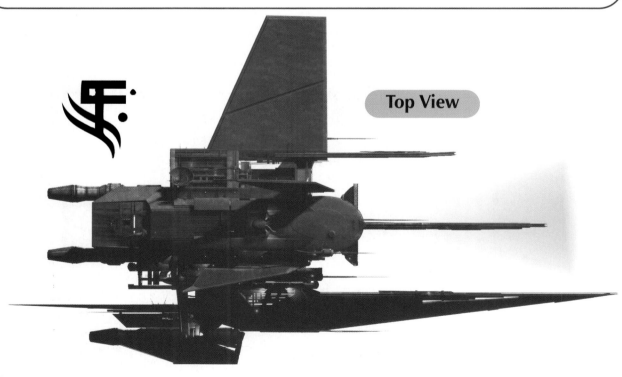

**Top View**

| | |
|---|---|
| **Length** | 490 meters |
| **Mass** | 27,000 tonnes |
| **Cruising Velocity** | 150 kps |
| **Max Velocity** | 200 kps |
| **Weapons** | 2 Turreted Lasers |
| | 10 Torpedo Tubes |
| | Light Fighter Complement |
| **Armor** | Fore and aft meson shields |
| | 32 cm fore/20 cm aft armor |
| | 26 cm port/starboard armor |

KILRATHI CAPITAL SHIP

**M14TCN5 Portable Data Reader Unit**

KILRATHI CAPITAL SHIP

# Fralthi-Class Cruiser

The Fralthi class seems to have been the primary battleship for inter-clan civil war for at least a century before the Kilrathi encountered humanity. In its basic configuration it has probably seen service for 150 years or more. Almost 2000 individual Fralthi-class ships have been identified in action, and several have been taken intact. Almost all Kilrathi fleet actions will involve at least one, and probably several, Fralthi.

The smallest Kilrathi ship to mount a carrier deck, the Fralthi class is capable of carrying a light squadron of about 50 fighters. With its three anti-matter main guns, it is very strong for its size in ship-to-ship actions, but carries a relatively small torpedo/missile loadout. It carries a complement of about 200 officers and crew, plus about 150 warriors.

Its engines are somewhat underpowered as compared to more recent Kilrathi ship designs, and it is both slow (in terms of top speed) and rather sluggish in its maneuvers. A Fralthi relies on its fighters and guns to repel an enemy, not on evasion or escape.

| | |
|---|---|
| *Length* | **475 meters** |
| *Mass* | **24,000 tonnes** |
| *Cruising Velocity* | **100 kps** |
| *Max Velocity* | **150 kps** |
| *Weapons* | **18 Point-Defense** |
| | **3 Antimatter Guns** |
| | **8 Torpedo Tubes** |
| | **Fighter Complement** |
| *Armor* | **Fore and aft meson shields** |
| | **28 cm fore armor** |
| | **18 cm aft armor** |
| | **22 cm port/starboard armor** |

Joan's has not yet acquired an accurate true-color image of a Fralthi-class cruiser. Our engineers have built the three-dimensional model below based on a synthesis of available intelligence.

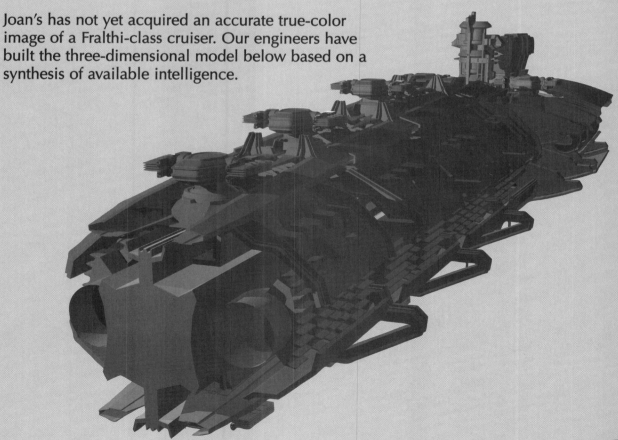

**KILRATHI CAPITAL SHIP**

**KILRATHI CAPITAL SHIP**

# Ralari-Class Destroyer

The Ralari-class destroyer represents the Kilrathi's sole known attempt at a warship with no fighter complement. Ralari-class ships are used for fleet defense, planetary assault and orbital defense. They predate the current conflict, but from their engineering it is believed that they are a relatively recent innovation for the Kilrathi. A Ralari's engines are extremely efficient, and it has above average speed and maneuverability for a ship its size. All Kilrathi task groups and escorted convoys include Ralari-class destroyers. Several thousand have been identified, and many intact specimens have been taken.

The Ralari holds a complement of about 150 officers and crew, plus a small unit of up to 50 warriors for use in marine operations. Although it doesn't have a fighter deck, a Ralari's standard complement includes three large transport shuttles, each capable of holding up to 100 armed warriors and their equipment. In invasion operations, they are often encountered in the presence of troop transports, with the Ralari acting as command and control for the landing operation.

The Ralari is also effective as a strategic bomber, and much of its cargo space is often devoted to ship-to-planet missile storage. Torpedoes, plus a remarkably heavy armament for a ship of its size, make it one of the most deadly Kilrathi vessels in ship-to-ship combat.

SCREEN 22 | subquery="kilrathi destroyer" | sort=bestmatch | return=all
source=joanships.mil.cap.kil.083952

**Side View**

| | |
|---:|:---|
| *Length* | 385 meters |
| *Mass* | 18,000 tonnes |
| *Cruising Velocity* | 150 kps |
| *Max Velocity* | 250 kps |
| *Weapons* | 2 Turreted Lasers |
| | 15 Point-Defense |
| | 2 Antimatter Guns |
| | 8 Torpedo Tubes |
| *Armor* | Fore and aft meson shields |
| | 25 cm fore/15 cm rear armor |
| | 20 cm port/starboard armor |

**Front View**

## KILRATHI CAPITAL SHIP

**MERCHANT VESSEL**

# Proxima Spaceworks Errant

The first Errants were produced in 2614, and the design has remained virtually unchanged since that time, aside from the addition of the optional-weapon hardpoints in 2621, incremental upgrades in the standard command and control software, and the evolution of the Hastings-Sakura drive array.

The lightest commercially available, jump-capable utility ship, the Proxima Errant is a workhorse of the Confed economy. The Errant is greatly valued for its modular construction and extreme customizability. Weapons and armor, for example, can be added and changed at will. The 10,000-cubic-meter hold can be fitted with a cabin module containing living space for one to four passengers (the unconfigured Errant includes cabin capacity for a crew of two, although only a single pilot is needed to operate the ship). By itself the Errant can be used effectively for light cargo, for passenger charter or as a courier, and it can even be customized for use as a recreational cabin cruiser. Its most common function, however, is as a control module for cargo drones or towed cargo units. Under its own power, an Errant has impulse capacity to effectively maneuver up to 20,000 tonnes of towed cargo. If its cargo units are independently powered, its capacity becomes effectively unlimited.

Front View

Top View

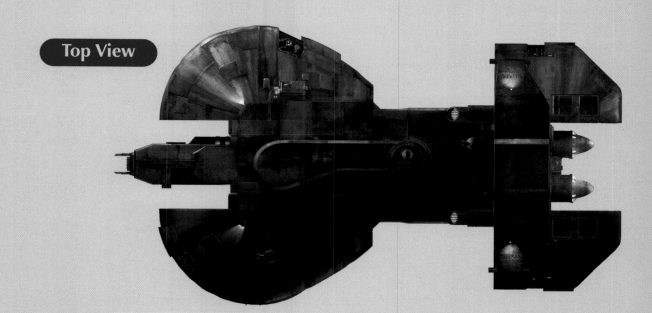

# MERCHANT VESSEL

|  |  |
|---:|:---|
| **Class** | Merchantman |
| **Length** | 25 meters |
| **Mass** | 100 tonnes |
| **Cruise Velocity** | 100 kps |
| **Max Velocity** | 150 kps |
| **Weapons** | 2 forward hardpoints |
|  | 1 turret hardpoint amidship |
| **Armor/Shields** | Optional |

**M14TCN5 Portable Data Reader Unit**

**CS** *TIGER CLAW*                                                    2654.074

Dear Mrs. Chen,

Please allow me to express my deepest sympathy on the death of your husband, Lt. Cmdr. Vince Chen, on behalf of the pilots and crew of the Tiger Claw.

Lt. Cmdr. Chen was an invaluable asset to this ship and this fighter wing. As I'm sure you know, he was known to his fellow pilots as "Bossman," and he was a natural leader within the squadron. The younger pilots all looked to him for instruction, and the officers in command listened carefully to his advice. As for myself, personally, I regarded him as a very close friend and trusted comrade. We shall all miss him profoundly.

I would like to relate the circumstances of Lt. Cmdr. Chen's death. Please be assured that he died in action, in accordance with the highest standards of Space Force honor and valor. I hope that this knowledge will be of some comfort to you and Lt. Cmdr. Chen's other loved ones.

On 2654.070 we were in LOCATION DELETED BY CONFED SECURITY system of the Roberts Quadrant, Vega Sector. The Tiger Claw was conducting sweeps of routes known to be frequented by Kilrathi spies and pirates. At 1600 hours, Lt. Commander Chen left the Tiger Claw in command of a wing of four Rapier fighters to conduct the regular afternoon patrol. At 1724 hours the wing detected and engaged a Kilrathi corvette guarded by three Dralthi escorts. The wing engaged the enemy, with Bossman accounting personally for two of the Dralthi, as well as coordinating the assault on the corvette, and were successful in destroying all ships with no losses. However, their ships were damaged in heavy fighting.

Two of the Rapiers had damage to weapons and communications systems. Bossman had only minor damage to hull armor. The fourth ship had damaged engines, and was unable to sustain normal cruising speed. Bossman sent the first two fighters back to the Tiger Claw at full speed (both landed safely), but remained to escort the fourth fighter.

At some point in the return trip, your husband met a Kilrathi patrol of four Dralthi. According to Bossman's flight recorder, the fighter he was escorting was destroyed early in the battle, but Bossman managed to destroy at least two, and possibly three, of the attackers. However, the enemy managed to damage his engines in such a way as to cause an overload in the reactor core. Your husband died of radiation poisoning from the core overload. The radiation was of sufficient intensity as to kill him instantly.

The Kilrathi did not make any attempt to salvage your husband's Rapier. We believe this is because the loss of their corvette made it difficult for them to take large prizes, and also because of the radiation hazard. Your husband's fighter was recovered and decontaminated, and his remains were buried at space. I trust you have already been informed of this.

There is one final fact about your husband's death that I feel you have the right to know. According to the flight recorder, your husband would have had time to eject between the damage to his engine and the radiation surge that killed him. I believe he chose to stay with his fighter in order to avoid the chance of being taken captive by the Kilrathi. Having some awareness of the Kilrathi's treatment of prisoners, I am in full agreement with your husband's choice.

At the time of his death, Lt. Cmdr. Chen had 30 confirmed fighter kills (including four confirmed kills on his final mission) and two confirmed cap ship kills. He was the third highest ranked ace in this squadron at the time of his death, by kill-count.

Lt. Cmdr. Chen could have saved himself by returning with the other two fighters and leaving the last to fend for itself. Instead, he chose to risk himself to protect a comrade. The captain has recommended that Lt. Cmdr. Chen be posthumously awarded the Red Comet, for pilots honorably killed in action, and his second Bronze Star for valor in the face of the enemy. I have enthusiastically endorsed these recommendations.

With profound sympathy,

*Lt. CMDR Jeanette Deveraux*

**LIEUTENANT COMMANDER JEANETTE DEVERAUX**
**SQUADRON COMMANDER, CS TIGER CLAW**

# Every Citizen's Guide to
# Practical Science

# STARSHIP DRIVES

*There are three basic types of modern starship drives.* **Impulse drive** *is the standard motive system for slower-than-light maneuvering for all star vehicles. The* **hopper drive** *is used to explore uncharted regions of space. The* **jump drive** *is used for instantaneous travel along pre-charted interstellar trade routes.*

## Impulse Drive

The earliest spacecraft were solid-propellant ballistic rockets. These behemoths needed tremendous quantities of fuel and were extremely limited in maneuverability. For space travel (even within a system) to become safe, practical and economical, a drive was needed that allowed a full range of maneuverability, used cheap, light and plentiful fuel, and could efficiently accelerate to speeds sufficient for regular inter-planetary travel. This need was answered by the development of a practical fusion engine in the mid-21st century. Both "hot" and "cold" fusion had been used in power plants for the cities of Terra for several decades by the time the technology became efficient enough to produce the first fusion-propelled prototype space vehicles. The first fusion craft, the *Sagan*, was commissioned by the UN Solar Trust in 2032, built by McDonnell-Douglas engineering, and launched from the L3 station in 2041. The *Sagan* flew a regular shuttle route between Luna, Mars and Titan for almost 75

years before it was finally decommissioned. (The original *Sagan* currently stands on Deimos, as part of the Spacefarer's Museum complex.)

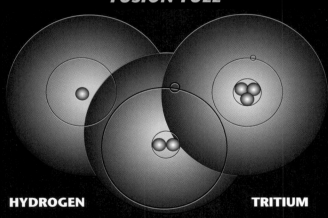

**FUSION FUEL**

**HYDROGEN**          **TRITIUM**

**DEUTERIUM**
**HYDROGEN ISOTOPES**

Fusion, or impulse, engines get much of their fuel from space itself, by sweeping up the gas that composes the "solar wind" produced by stars.

The impulse engine actually consists of two elements. The first is, of course, the engine itself. This consists of electromagnetic field generators, usually mounted at the stern of the ship. Hydrogen gas is released into the field created by these generators, where it is compressed with a force comparable to that in the center of a star. The compression creates "hot fusion," the same process that creates and maintains stars. (This is related to, but very different from, the "cold fusion" used by the energy cells that power nearly all modern equipment.) That energy, in turn, propels the spacecraft. Large freighters and battleships usually operate under a thrust of one, or at most two, standard gravities, while light fighters and couriers can sustain a thrust of up to 8G. This same fusion reaction also provides power for the ship's life support, communications, weapons, shields and other systems. (Most ships, small and large, back up these peripheral systems with an array of standard cold-impulse cells, for emergency use.)

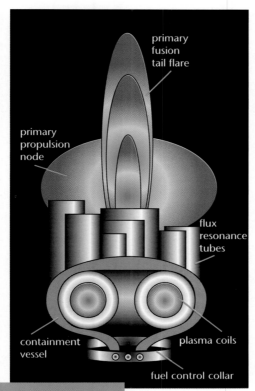

primary fusion tail flare

primary propulsion node

flux resonance tubes

containment vessel

plasma coils

fuel control collar

**Ramscoop**

The second element of an impulse engine is the ramscoop. This also consists of electromagnetic field generators—in fact, small ships use the same generators to create both fields. The ramscoop field, projected for up to several kilometers around and ahead of the ship, sweeps hydrogen gas into large intakes in the bow of the ship, where it is filtered and stored in the ship's fuel tank. The faster a ship goes, the more fuel gets swept into the tank. At low speeds, the amount of fuel swept up is fairly insignificant. At high speeds, the fuel is enough to maintain the ship's engines indefinitely, without ever "dipping into" the tank. A ship must always use tanked fuel for acceleration, but once at speed it can rely on ramscoop intake for operation. A very large ship moving at moderate speeds actually sweeps up more gas than it uses, and can recharge its tanks as it flies; small ships like fighters and shuttles usually run at a slight deficit, and must refuel from their carrier or a tanker.

One side effect of the ramscoop is drag—sweeping up the gas actually acts to slow down the ship. This drag increases the faster the ship goes, and must be countered by thrust. Thus, ships have a maximum speed based on their thrust and size, and cannot accelerate beyond this speed. The maximum speed of a bulky freighter or a cap ship, for instance, is about 150 kps; for a sleek fighter, it's up to 500 kps. When a ship shuts off its engines, it slowly loses headway.

Small ships like starfighters and racers, for whom speed is a premium, have "afterburners" that adjust the ramscoop field. The opening of the field is reduced, to reduce drag, and the gas is routed past the ship rather than into the tanks. At the stern, the ramscoop field captures and compresses the gas to fusion, acting like an extra set of engines. The result is 50% more thrust and a nearly doubled top speed. However, no fuel is being swept into the tanks—using afterburners rapidly depletes the small fuel tanks that fighters carry.

If a ship doesn't need to maneuver, it can reduce the size of the ramscoop field while maintaining normal thrust. This reduces drag and drastically increases the ship's maximum speed. However, ships maneuver by manipulating the engines' fields to redirect the exhaust. The higher the thrust (and therefore speed), the higher the maneuvering thrust required. Thus, ships only use reduced-scoop speeds when they do not expect to need to maneuver, such as when traveling between worlds. In this one respect, impulse-drive ships are much like the ancient "rockets" that proceeded them—for maximum speed and efficiency, they must plot out their course in advance, and head for it with a minimum of maneuvering.

M14TCN5 Portable Data Reader Unit

The complex electromagnetic fields used by engines and ramscoops are created by "magnetic monopoles." These are like regular magnets, except that where a normal magnet has two poles (north and south), a monopole has only one pole (either north or south). Most monopoles are very weak; they are used like amplifiers to control and redirect much larger fields produced by standard electromagnets. Monopoles are an artifact left over from the Big Bang, billions of years ago, and can no longer be created in the normal universe; they are thus a very valuable commodity, and the focus of much exploration outside the normal space routes.

The complexity of a ship determines how many monopoles are required; the mass and size of the ship determines how powerful each monopole must be. Thus, a starfighter requires thirty microgauss (30 millionths of a gauss) monopoles; a cruiser or free trader needs a dozen milligauss (12 thousandths of a gauss) monopoles; a large passenger liner requires four centigauss (four 100ths of a gauss) monopoles.

## Gravitic Warp Theory

Hopper and jump drives are still popularly referred to as faster-than-light (FTL) drives, but this is a misnomer. As Einstein predicted, it remains impossible for an object made of normal matter to accelerate beyond the speed of light in this universe. However, gravitic warping—the principle behind both the hopper and the jump drive—makes possible something that's even more incredible . . . the instantaneous transition of matter from one point in the universe to another, far different point.

The Grand Unified Theory, perfected in the late 2000s, led to the development of antigravity vehicles. Unlike modern "antigravity" vehicles, which simply divert and channel gravity, these vehicles actually negated gravity, by projecting a field in which the gravitic mass of every particle was suppressed. This meant that the occupants of the vehicle were weightless, and thus subject to all the inconveniences and discomforts that condition causes. Naturally, there was immense commercial pressure to develop a more comfortable alternative.

In 2214, Dr. Shari Akwende, a subatomic engineer working for Aerospatiale Afrique, was searching for a solution to that exact problem. The Grand Unified Theory implied the existence of antigravitons, counterparts to the gravitons that carried the gravitic force. These antigravitons have half-lives of many microseconds—very short in "real-world" terms, but quite long in the subatomic field. Like many researchers of the time, Akwende assumed that generating a sufficient constant antigraviton flux would push something away, in the same way that graviton flux pulled things toward the generator. This would result in vehicles that were no more weightless than 20th-century airplanes, but that retained all the advantages of antigravity.

Akwende had already made a significant advance, putting her years ahead of competitors. She had conclusively determined that matter-antimatter collisions conducted in a suppressed-gravity field would produce antigravitons. But so far, her antigraviton generator had produced no thrust whatsoever, in spite of generating what was, in theory, a large enough flux. In the course of trying to detect any thrust at all, Akwende discovered that the antigravitons showed a very slight tendency to head in a single direction. That direction changed over the course of the year, and when correlated with Earth's motion, pointed in the rough direction of Alpha Centauri. Repeating the experiments on an early Plutonian flight enabled Akwende to triangulate on the exact point in space, a small patch between the orbits of Pluto and Neptune, where the antigravitons were heading. It would be several decades before the ability to produce antigravitons would bear fruit, and centuries before the implications of Akwende's "antigraviton flow" would be realized.

## SCREEN 4 | query "jump physics, layman" level=UNCLASSIFIED
## source=1st ed. cit publ, Practical Science, TERRA, 2651

Even today, only a small fraction of the gravitic warp theory is truly understood. There are three competing theories, each of which requires the suspension of a different fundamental law. However, a large body of empirical research has been compiled, and the effect can be described, if not understood. The basic concepts of gravitic warping are usually described as follows.

Stretch a large cloth, like a bedspread, tight. Now put two rocks on it, some distance apart. You'll notice that each rock is sitting at the bottom of a deep dimple in the sheet. If they're close enough together, the two dimples intersect, with a saddle-shaped "ridge" in between them. If you put a marble next to one of the rocks and push it hard enough toward the other one, it will roll up out of the dimple, across the ridge, and down into the other dimple, winding up next to the second rock.

Take the whole assembly and start lowering it into a pool, keeping the cloth stretched tight. Stop when the two rocks are just covered in water. Everything is the same, except that the water slows down the marble, and it becomes much harder to push it up out of the dimples. In fact, for the sake of this discussion, we'll say it's now impossible to push the rock out of the dimples. So, to repeat the marble trick, you'll have to start with the marble out of the water, but still on a line between the two rocks.

Replace the bedspread with deep space, the rocks with stars and the marble with a starship, and you've got a fairly good model of jump travel. The pool is the "antigraviton potential field," and the water level the "Olivarez equilibrium boundary," but we'll call it sea level.

Remember that we've replaced the imaginary two-dimensional bedspread with three-dimensional

space. Those of us trapped inside that space view it as flat. So rather than seeing "sea level" as some line above our heads, we see it as a sphere enclosing each star at a constant radius. (To picture this, take the bedspread out of the water and take the rocks away. You've got two large wet circles.) If we draw a line from one star to another, we'll find the jump points at the precise intersections of the "sea level" sphere and that line.

Or at least we would, if space had just two stars. But even this one galaxy has billions of stars, and

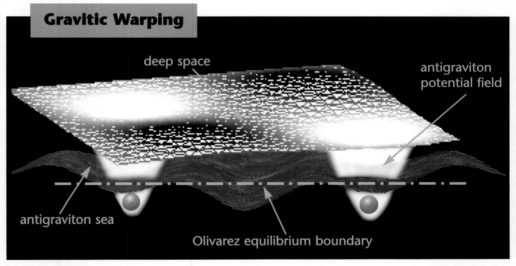

**Gravitic Warping**

deep space

antigraviton potential field

antigraviton sea

Olivarez equilibrium boundary

nearly every star has planets, and the gaps between the stars are filled with gas and dust and rocks. Every single piece of matter, right down to a single gas molecule, makes its own dimple in the bedspread—and every piece of matter is moving, so the dimples wander around. What that means is that the line between the two stars is not precisely straight, nor is it constant or even predictable. So the intersections of that line and sea level move around. Plus, sea level isn't constant—the planets have their own, moving dimples that make the sea-level sphere irregular. There's even evidence pointing to the existence of "tides" in the antigraviton sea, adding to the variation in sea level.

Back to our bedspread. The closer together the two rocks are, the closer to the water the ridge is. In fact, if the rocks are heavy enough, and close

**M14TCN5 Portable Data Reader Unit**

enough together, the ridge will be underwater. No jump line. On the other hand, if the rocks are light enough, they won't dip into the water at all. Again, no jump line.

This is a place where the analogy breaks down a little. The marble views the water as nothing but a hindrance. The jump ship, however, needs the antigraviton potential—it needs the exact right amount, not too much or too little. That's why the big stars have more jump points than the small ones—they dip deeper into the antigraviton well.

Now we'll mix metaphors. If something large enough to dip below sea level passes between two stations, it sets up a new station. Jump ships will find themselves arriving at an unexpected destination and having to survey out the second jump point to continue. This is why jump flights are occasionally delayed—the jumps themselves are still instantaneous, but the ship has to take time at the "transfer station." If the intervening body is too close to one of the stations for a jump line, then the jump ship has no choice but to return to port and wait until the "weather" clears.

This phenomenon, called "equipotential eclipsing," happens more frequently than one might expect, since jump lines aren't straight. The lines can twist every which way, following the contours of space. Bodies heavy enough to eclipse a jump line—and something as small as Luna can do it—are also heavy enough to attract the line toward themselves.

Let's change the bedspread a little. Make it out of plastic instead of cloth. Now it returns to its normal flat condition more slowly. When we roll a marble across a ridge, the marble makes its own dimple as it moves. The bedspread takes time to resume its normal shape after the marble has passed.

Our marble analogy has one major flaw. A jump ship doesn't actually move. It doesn't cross the intervening space the way the marble rolls along the ridge. The ridge line is a physical thing that the marble follows. The jump line is a fictional construct that helps us predict where (and whether!) the jump ship will arrive. The passage of the marble warps the bedspread behind it; thus,

the marble has no effect on its own journey, but only on the journeys of marbles that attempt to follow it. A jump ship's journey, however, is instantaneous. There is no "before" or "after"—the ship warps the jump line, and if the line shifts its endpoint, then that endpoint is where the ship reappears. And if the line vanishes altogether, then so does the ship.

Jump ships are safe because jump pilots are careful, not because jump travel itself is safe. Quite the contrary, jump travel is almost insanely dangerous. The speed of light is one of the universe's most fundamental physical laws, and it only barely tolerates our violating it. If we push against the limits of jump travel even slightly, we are immediately punished for our temerity.

## Hopper Drives

Hopper drives—more formally Morvan drives (named after Dr. Andre Morvan, 2288 – 2336, who first hypothesized their feasibility) or antigraviton pulse generators—were the first working "FTL" engines created by humanity. The early prototypes appeared late in the 22nd century.

We've already described how gravity distorts space. This is true not only of normal gravity, generated by massive physical objects, but also true of large concentrations of antigraviton particles. Such concentrations very seldom occur in nature (see p. 52), but they can be created. A sufficiently large matter/antimatter reaction, taking place in space far removed from any strong gravity fields, will create a local and very temporary "space warp" in its immediate area.

To visualize how this fits in with the "dimpled sheet" analogy for space-time, imagine that space is a strong but very flexible rubber sheet covering a liquid medium. Drop a small but very heavy object on the sheet, and you will get a deep, narrow dimple in the sheet. Because the sheet is rubber, it will eventually return to its original position (or close to it), but because it's stretched over a liquid medium (scientists refer to this medium as "subspace," and its existence is still highly theoretical), until the sheet returns to normal that medium will simultaneously try to flow into the "well" created by the dropped object. If the "well" is deep and narrow enough, the pressure of the liquid will actually cause the mouth of the well to close for an instant, allowing an object at the precise correct spot on the sheet to move instantly from one point to another via the closed-off mouth of the well. To "hop" across, as it were.

The hopper drive involves setting a powerful, but tightly focused matter-antimatter reaction, generating enough antigravitons to create a temporary space-time "well."

If a ship is correctly positioned at the very edge of the reaction's event horizon, it can hop across space instantaneously. This "warp" is localized, so the amount of space that can be crossed by it is strictly limited — most hops involve a distance of 20% to 35% of a light-year.

Obviously, it takes many such hops to transit the distance between even relatively close stars. Nonetheless, the hopper ship can move across space at an average effective rate of up to 10 times the speed of light (that is, if two stars systems are 10 light-years apart, an efficient hopper ship can move between them in about a year). Although hopper technology makes star travel possible, voyages still take a significant time in relation to the human lifespan. Therefore, hopper-ships are sometimes called "sloships."

Hopper drives are extremely dangerous. If the ship is positioned even a tiny fraction too close to the reaction, it will be "in the well" when the warp closes, confined with the full force of the reaction—which will certainly annihilate it down to the subatomic level. (This same principle is used offensively to create gravitic mines.) Furthermore the reaction must be triggered far from any large gravity-generating objects. Otherwise, gravitic distortion from these objects will prevent the well from ever closing at all, once again exposing the ship to the force of the reaction. (The safe distance from Sol system for a hop, for example, is about 1.25 times the outer limits of Pluto's orbit, assuming Pluto, Uranus, and Neptune are all at points in their orbits well away from the chosen point.)

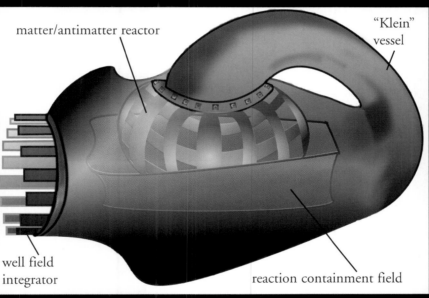

matter/antimatter reactor

"Klein" vessel

well field integrator

reaction containment field

**HOPPER DRIVE**

Hopper drives are "slow," because time must pass between each hop. Hops can not be ventured less than 18 hours apart, and most captains will not try more than one per standard day. (Local conditions might delay hops much longer.) Lenghty intervals between hops are necessary because of the time it takes to place a reaction-charge and calculate the event horizon, because of the time needed for a ram scoop to generate the energy needed for a hop, but most importantly it's necessary because hops disturb space time. Once a hop takes place, both time and distance are necessary to get to a place where space is sufficiently "quiet" to hop again.

The earliest interstellar colonists and traders used hopper drives because that was the only technology they had. Today most star-traffic uses the less dangerous and more economical jump drive—hopper drives are reserved for explorer and deep-space patrol craft.

**M14TCN5 Portable Data Reader Unit**

## Jump Drives

The jump drive is the basic medium of modern interstellar commerce. It allows instantaneous transit between star systems. It is both safer and more powerful than the hopper drive, because it uses natural, stable jump points between the stars instead of creating dangerous and temporary local distortions in space-time—the "grooves" in space-time produced by powerful gravitational fields.

Not every jump point is useful. Since heavier objects naturally produce more jump lines, most jump lines run to or between super-heavy stars, far too massive to support any sort of planetary system. (These stars, however, are often used as "way stations" on trips between systems.) One additional advantage that jump drives have over the hopper drive is that jump points often exist relatively near stars—jump points are typically far closer to the orbits of habitable planets than the nearest approach possible via hopper drive.

The jump drive is formally known as the "Akwende drive," after Sheri Akwende, the discoverer of antigraviton drift. It is this drift that allows us to detect, locate and ultimately transit jump points. The first jump drives were created by Pilgrims about 150 years ago, but they kept its existence secret from the Confed government. The first working Confed prototype was installed on the *Haile Selassie*, which made a successful jump-transit from Sol to Polaris on 2588.315, returning on .323.

A jump-ship has three essential components. The first is an Akwende drive itself. The drive is usually mounted in the center of the ship, securely braced. The second is a set of fusion engines, for maneuvering to and from jump points. The third is a containment vessel of antiprotons, fuel for the antigraviton generator. Most large ships also carry the equipment to create more antiprotons and recharge the tank, but this isn't strictly necessary.

To begin a journey, the jump ship must first find the jump point. In settled systems, the jump points are carefully charted and tracked—a ship will know what section of space to search, but it must search nevertheless. To find a jump point, the drive is switched on at a very low level, producing a slow trickle of antigravitons. Sensing equipment around the edges of the drive determines where the antigravitons are leading. All jump ships are fitted with this equipment, but most civilian craft can only home in on jump points when they're already within a few hundred thousand kilometers (i.e., they have to know—very exactly, by the scale of interstellar space—where the jump point is before they can head for it). Military or exploration vessels can plot jump points across many millions of kilometers.

Once the location of the point is determined, the ship starts its fusion engines and heads towards it. As the ship gets closer to the jump point, the attraction of the antigravitons toward the point becomes stronger and stronger. When the ship is close enough to the point that the antigravitons can actually arrive at the point itself before decaying (a distance of about 500 meters), the jump drive starts to produce real thrust, though at this point that thrust is very small.

The ship stops at the edge of the jump area to get a precise bearing on the jump point, including its drift rate. It then kicks in the engines, gets as close as possible to the jump point, and activates the jump drive at full power. The high thrust provided by the jump drive drags the ship to the exact jump point. Once the source of antigravitons coincides with the jump point, an antigraviton field is created with a roughly 500-meter radius. (The radius is a constant, based on the half-life of antigravitons.) If the intensity of this field is sufficient, based on the mass contained within the field and the speed with which that mass is moving, then everything in the field vanishes at the point of departure and arrives at the point of arrival, keeping all its original momentum.

All parts of the jump-ship must be subjected to roughly the same amount of antigraviton flux. Because of the short lifespan of these particles, this effectively translates into a maximum ship radius of about 500 meters. Since particles have a half-life, this radius is not fixed, and to a certain extent the power of the drive determines the radius of the sphere. Ships bigger in radius than 500 meters take vastly more power than ones smaller than this threshold. If a ship is too big for its antigraviton flux, then only the parts that are within the field complete the jump—meaning parts of the ship may be left behind, with possibly disastrous results.

Since the speed of the ship affects the amount of antigravitons required to initiate the jump, a ship can reduce the jump's energy needs by carefully maneuvering to the exact location of the jump point, and matching vectors with the jump point's drift, before turning on the drive. This results in the minimum-energy jump for a given mass, but can take quite some time to achieve. However, for ships that are close to the maximum size, this is the safest way to make a jump.

Each jump draws energy out of the jump line used. This energy is proportional to the energy required to initiate the jump. Thus, a minimum-energy jump takes less energy out of the jump line. Reducing the energy of a jump line may make it connect to a new destination, or it may disconnect it entirely. When a ship attempts a jump that depletes the line's energy, it will either arrive at the wrong destination, or it will simply disappear. No one knows where ships that vanish this way go; they are presumed destroyed.

When a ship generates more antigraviton energy than it needs for the jump, the excess is dissipated in a burst of light and neutrinos at both ends of the jump. This burst is easily detectable from long range. If the ship takes time to calculate the exact amount of energy required, and is equipped with a "variable-flux engine," it can make a "stealth" jump, eliminating the flash at both ends. Under normal conditions, ships seldom bother with this; in fact, few civilian ships are even equipped with the gear necessary to calculate the antigraviton flux.

As has been mentioned several times, the jump takes no time at all, in either the frame of reference of the jump ship or that of an outside observer at either end. The only time required for jump travel is that of traveling to and from jump points.

## Between Scylla and Charybdis

Ancient mariners told tales of a strait passage guarded by two mythical monsters. Scylla was a huge, many-headed monster that liked to pluck hapless sailors off the decks of their ship, while Charybdis was a great, all-devouring whirlpool. If you tried to navigate the straits to avoid the arms of Scylla, you would be sucked into the maw of Charybdis, while if you tried to sail around the whirlpool, you came within reach of the monster.

The modern Scylla and Charybdis don't guard some ancient Aegean trade route, they guard the final leg of the Ulysses corridor—the longest, and most dangerous, currently charted jump line, which stretches from the outer Sol system to the remote edge of Vega Sector. And they're not monsters of legend, they're two of the universe's most exotic natural phenomena.

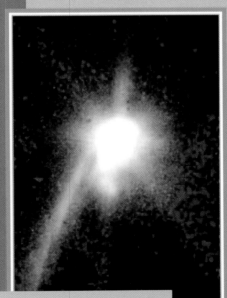

Charybdis, the most spectacular light show in the known galaxy, showing its all-devouring whirlpool.

In the remote outskirts of the Vega Sector not far from the Kilrathi border, Charybdis is actually the more normal of the two. It is a quasar, a rapidly expanding star that emits light as lasers, and the most spectacular light show in the known galaxy. Quasars and pulsars (i.e., rotating neutron stars) are notoriously prolific generators of jump points. Their agitated movements (the pulsar's rotation, the quasar's expansion) cause dramatic distortions in the space-time fabric, distortions that are the structural basics of a jump line.

The difference between a pulsar's jump points and a quasar's, is that the pulsar's are shifting constantly according to laws of quantum indeterminacy. Theoretically you can get to (or at least close ) anywhere in the universe from the pulsar. The rawback is that it's impossible to predict where

expansion, as well as to the sheer number of jump points around the star, the points tend to "jostle" each other constantly, making them hard to find and impossible to predict. It's a matter of historical record, however, that Pilgrims have jumped quasars, and Confed scientists are still trying to uncover the navigational secrets that made this possible.

As quasars go, Charybdis is not a particularly exceptional specimen. Its companion, however, is a true enigma. The Scylla anomaly is one of the most mysterious phenomenon in all of explored space, and it lies almost within reach (astronomcally speaking) of humanity's birthplace, in the Oort cloud of Sol system, beyond the reaches of Pluto, where comets make their slow preparations for their long fall inward. Like one of the great monsters of horror fiction, Scylla is a Thing That Should Not Be. Scientists call it a "gravitic anomaly," but that just explains what it does. Nobody knows what it really is.

Scylla is a compressed field of gravity as strong as the largest star. An object that dense, that close to the sun, should behave like a second, dark sun turning Sol system into a binary star system (and ripping most of the system's planets and moons apart). However, Scylla has little if any effect on surrounding space (although some feel it may be responsible for the irregularity of Pluto's orbit). In fact, like the Scylla from myth, it's almost undetectable until you're already in its grip. Even if you are 100,000 kilometers from Scylla, you won't know it's there (unless you are looking with some extremely specialized equipment), but pass within 30,000 k of the beast and you'll be in her clutches sucked down into the singularity at her core and reduced to your component sub-atomic particles.

Sol Sector | Vega Sector

Charybdis

SOL | VEGA

Enigma Sector | Epsilon Sector

● **Charybdis theoretical jump points**

ou'll end up. (Pilgrim legends say that they had avigators who had the mystical power to jump ulsars, but most Confed scientists dismiss the ccounts as simple myth.) Pulsar jump points also nd to appear at an inconvenient depth in the ulsar's massive gravity well.

A quasar, like Charybdis, also has thousands of stinct jump points, but they're more stable than pulsar's. Once a quasar jump point comes into xistence, it tends to remain in existence, and on- ne to the same spot. This makes it theoretically ossible to jump quasars, but that doesn't mean oing so is either safe or easy. Most stable jump oints lie a convenient, sensible distance from the ar that created them, and drift lazily about in a edictable fashion. Quasars, however, are con- antly expanding. This has the effect of keeping eir jump points dangerously near the corona of e star (and quasar coronas, with their constant ser emissions, are even less safe than the coronas most stars). Also due to the quasar's rapid

## Gravity is not supposed to work like this.

Here's scientists' best guess at how Scylla works: the Unified Field Theorem states that gravitons, which create gravity, are opposed by antigravitons. Gravitons are generated by any object with mass—the more massive the object, the greater the gravity. Antigravitons are much rarer in the physical universe. They can be generated by specific sorts of matter/antimatter reactions, or by some very exotic stellar phenomena.

Scylla seems to be a singularity emitting massive quantities of both gravitons and antigravitons in equilibrium. The antigravitons naturally "float to the top," creating a field around the anomaly that cancels out the deadly pull of the gravitons immediately around the singularity. Pass Scylla

This describes what Scylla does, but scientists still have no idea why it exists. Some think it may be some kind of black hole gone wrong, somehow put "in reverse" to emit particles instead of absorbing them. Others throw up their hands and declare that Scylla could not possibly exist naturally, so it must be an artifact of some ancient civilization that deliberately put it there on the outskirts of Sol's system. Everybody agrees that the particles emitted from Scylla must originate in another universe, but exactly what that means in this context is the subject of hot debate.

Pilgrim explorers are said to have performed dangerous tricks with Scylla, "surfing" the interface between the graviton mass and the antigraviton field to do high-speed "slingshot" maneuvers towards the inner planets. Then there's Scylla's one jump point, a portal to the longest jump line known to man. Advocates of the "alien construct" theory of Scylla's origin say that that may be why it was made in the first place, to create an exceptionally long and stable jump line. If so, that still leaves unanswered the question of who these aliens were, and why they needed an express route from Sol to the wilderness of Vega.

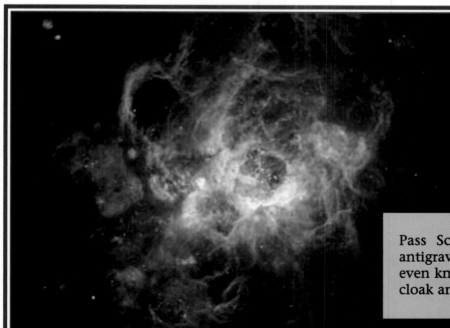

Pass Scylla without entering its antigraviton "cloak" and you won't even know it's there, but pierce the cloak and the monster has you.

without entering her antigraviton "cloak" (which is about 1,000 k thick and spreads itself out at about the aforementioned 30,000 k mark from the center) and you won't even know it's there; but pierce the cloak and the monster has you.

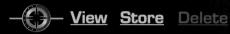

View  Store  Delete

### PILOT NOSE ART
**Each pilot that enters Confed services leaves a recognizable mark on the Flight Deck . . .**

View  Store  Delete

### PILOT REVIEWS: *CS TIGER CLAW*
**It is privilege to report that Lt. Christopher Blair has graduated Fighter Pilot training with Distinction . . .**

View  Store  Delete

### MARINE BOARDING PROTOCOL
**A *boarding operation* is an operation wherein a boarding party is inserted into a vessel known or suspected to be under enemy control . . .**

View  Store  Delete

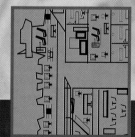

### DECK PLANS: CS *TIGER CLAW*
**A Bengal-class carrier, the CS *Tiger Claw* can transport 550 crew members and 104 spacecraft . . .**

View   Store   Delete

# FLIGHT DECK PROTOCOL

**The following instructions apply to all person-nel on the Flight Deck. If you don't understand these rules, do not enter the deck. . . .**

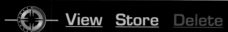
View   Store   Delete

# CASUALTIES AMONG 88TH FIGHTER WING

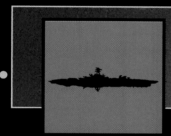

View   Store   Delete

# COMMON CONFED & KILRATHI SHIPS PROPORTIONAL SIZE & SILHOUETTE RECOGNITION CHART

View   Store   Delete

# KILRATHI TACTICS

**In planning effective offensive and defensive oper-ations against the Kilrathi, it is first necessary to . . .**

uery "confidential update" media=org_class, level=**CONFIDENTIAL** | eturn=8 . . . Retrieving 8 text files + graphical subfiles . . . Keying search 881CU. Please insert data chip . . . You may view, store, or delete.

article 1 of 8="pilot nose art, cs tiger claw"
article 2 of 8="pilot reviews, cs tiger claw"
article 3 of 8="boarding protocol, confed marines"
article 4 of 8="deck plans, cs tiger claw"
article 5 of 8="flight deck protocol, confed naval"
article 6 of 8="casualties, 88th fighter wing"
article 7 of 8="ship silhouettes (relative sizes)"
article 8 of 8="kilrathi tactics"

CONFIDENTIAL

**M14TCN5 Portable Data Reader Unit**

SEARCH PREV NEXT RELOAD SAVE PRINT QUIT

**SCREEN 1** | query "lt blair, cs tiger claw" media=archives/confid
level=CONFIDENTIAL | source=TCSF Flight School, SIRIUS, 2654

**CSF FLIGHT SCHOOL**

## Final Evaluation, Lt. Christopher Blair

**To: Captain Sansky, CS Tiger Claw**
**From: Major E. Gonsalas, C.O. 145th Training Wing, CSF Flight School, Sirius**

*SIR,*
*It is privilege to report that Lt. Christopher Blair has graduated Fighter Pilot training with Distinction, as a member of the Q1 class of 2654, and has been assigned to your vessel's Fighter Squadron. As Lt. Blair's flight instructor, I have prepared the following summation of his capabilities.*

### ACADEMY RECORD

| | |
|---|---|
| GPA 3.64 | Rank in Class 477 (of 1403) |
| **Flight School Academic Record** | |
| GPA 4.22 | Rank in Class 23 (of 314) |
| **Flight School Flight Record** | |
| Flight 96.2 | Rank in Class 1 (of 314) |
| Marksmanship 93.4 | Rank in Class 2 (of 314) |
| Safety 100 (0 accidents, 0 ships lost) | Rank in Class 1 (of 314) |
| Navigation 100 | Rank in Class 1 (of 314) |

Blair is reserved among others, but when he speaks up at all he tends to speak his mind. He does not welcome personal questions. Although not a natural leader, his talents in flight point to strong leadership potential within a flight unit. He accepts criticism well when it's directly related to performance of his duties. Blair will do best in an environment where policies are clearly set forth, but pilots are allowed a reasonable degree of mission autonomy.

### STRENGTHS

• Astonishing control and discipline in the cockpit.

• Deep sense of personal ethics.

### WEAKNESSES

• Independent thinking may lead to the appearance of questioning orders.

• Sensitive to comments about his family. Blair is an orphan, and inappropriate remarks about his parents may lead to tension, particularly under battle pressure.

### SUMMATION

Lt. Blair is simply one of the most gifted young pilots I have ever trained or flown with. His composite flight score (97.4) is a new record high among pilots coming to Flight School directly from the Academy. Furthermore, he is the first graduate of this institution to ever achieve a perfect score in Navigation. In flight, Blair is confident, focused, disciplined and creative. He understands teamwork, but performs best when allowed to take the initiative.

### ADDENDUM

Since Lts. Blair and Marshall are both being assigned to your ship (as per my recommendation) I am attaching this addendum to both pilots' evaluations.

In training, Blair and Marshall were both close friends and personal rivals. They respect and trust one another, and there is little doubt that each brings out the best in the other. In flight, they make a remarkable team, but they do display a regrettable tendency to assume that as a team they are unbeatable, which will need to be beaten out of them if they are to reach their full potential as a flight team.

Both Blair and Marshall are already blooded in combat. During a routine training flight they surprised and destroyed a Kilrathi blockade-runner. During this action against a superior force, both pilots displayed skill, courage and discipline normally found only in more experienced warriors. It is because of this remarkable achievement that I recommended Blair and Marshall be assigned together for their first combat tour.

## CSF FLIGHT SCHOOL

## Final Evaluation, Lt. Todd Marshall

**To: Captain Sansky, CS Tiger Claw**
**From: Major E. Gonsalas, C.O. 145th Training Wing, CSF Flight School, Sirius**

*SIR,*
*It is privilege to report that Lt. Todd Marshall has graduated Fighter Pilot training with Recognition, as a member of the Q1 class of 2654, and has been assigned to your vessel's Fighter Squadron. As Lt. Marshall's flight instructor, I have prepared the following summation of his current capabilities.*

### ACADEMY RECORD

| | |
|---|---|
| GPA 4.02 | Rank in Class 125 (of 1403) |
| **Flight School Academic Record** | |
| GPA 4.50 | Rank in Class 9 (of 314) |
| **Flight School Flight Record** | |
| Flight 91.1 | Rank in Class 2 (of 314) |
| Marksmanship 95.1 | Rank in Class 1 (of 314) |
| Safety 64 *(3 accidents, 1 ships lost, inquiry found no fault)* | Rank in Class 311 (of 314) |
| Navigation 88 | Rank in Class 22 (of 314) |

Among others, Marshall is outgoing and generally likable, but may create tension with a flash of temper or inappropriate "wit." He shows tremendous long-term leadership potential, but needs a more mature outlook before being given actual command authority. He accepts suggestions well, but can become defensive if directly criticized. Marshall needs a highly disciplined, structured environment. He needs to fly with experienced, skilled pilots that he can look up to.

### STRENGTHS

- Extremely gifted, fearless pilot.
- Tremendous talent for finding unconventional solutions.

### WEAKNESSES

- Takes unnecessary risks. Tends to trivialize personal danger.
- Doesn't always know when to shut up.

### SUMMATION

Lt. Marshall is a pilot of infinite promise. His Flight and Marksmanship scores, as well as his classroom grades, are exemplary. In flight, Marshall is aggressive, creative and committed. Although cleared of any charges in the three accidents he was involved in during training, Marshall undeniably tends towards a high-risk, seat-of-his-pants flying style. Although his offensive instincts are highly developed, he sometimes forgets that his wingmen may not be as on top of the situation as he is (hopefully this will be less of a factor with more experienced pilots). This is a significant drawback to Marshall's otherwise excellent teamwork skills. His single biggest drawback as a pilot is a tendency to see combat as a game or challenge, rather than a life-or-death struggle.

### ADDENDUM

Since Lts. Blair and Marshall are both being assigned to your ship (as per my recommendation) I am attaching this addendum to both pilots' evaluations.

In training, Blair and Marshall were both close friends and personal rivals. They respect and trust one another, and there is little doubt that each brings out the best in the other. In flight, they make a remarkable team, but they do display a regrettable tendency to assume that as a team they are unbeatable, which will need to be beaten out of them if they are to reach their full potential as a flight team.

Both Blair and Marshall are already blooded in combat. During a routine training flight they surprised and destroyed a Kilrathi blockade-runner. During this action against a superior force, both pilots displayed skill, courage and discipline normally found only in more experienced warriors. It is because of this remarkable achievement that I recommended Blair and Marshall be assigned together for their first combat tour.

SCREEN 1 | query "lt cmdr deveraux, cs tiger claw" media=archives/confid
level=CONFIDENTIAL | source=CS Tiger Claw bi-annual pilot eval

## BI-ANNUAL PILOT EVALUATION

**CS TIGER CLAW**
*Executive Office*
**Commander Paul Gerald, 2654.02**

### Lt. Commander Jeanette Deveraux (callsign Angel)
### Squadron Commander

### PERFORMANCE

As a pilot, Lt. Cmdr. Deveraux has few equals aboard the Tiger Claw. She has a crisp, clean flying style and a thorough understanding of battle situations.

As a commander, Angel has been an exemplary squadron commander, and in my opinion we are fortunate to have her aboard. In the past year, she has single-handedly managed to turn around a defeatist and enervating morale situation aboard the Tiger Claw. When she was promoted to her current duties, the sick time was high, fire-to-hit ratios were low, and the pilot return rate was one of the lowest in the fleet.

At the time of this evaluation, the situation is reversed. Sick leave seems nearly restricted to critical situations, due primarily to ongoing sim contests and maneuver drills. She has taught her pilots the real-world necessity of "book flying" and teamwork.

She's also led her pilots, by example, to take personal pride in the maintenance of their fighters. Now all ships are competently double-checked by the pilots. Efficiency ratings in the Repair Pit have doubled in the last six months.

### LEADERSHIP

Unlike many commanders, Lt. Cmdr. Deveraux does not use sympathy or camaraderie to inspire her pilots. In fact, many people—including both subordinates and peers—have complained of her "cold demeanor" and lack of compassion. Her methods are effective, however. She drills her people until their skills begin to develop, and never misses the opportunity to provide positive reinforcement for improvement. The fact that she is also quick to reprimand, and has a scathing wit to aim at anyone who doesn't work up to his fullest potential, provides the sharp "stick" to counterpoint any of her "carrot" compliments.

### ACTION POINTS

I am concerned about Lt. Cmdr. Deveraux's encouragement of the custom that pilots "disremember" any battle fatalities. It may be a way of coping with the high mortality rate, but the captain and I are concerned that it is not psychologically healthy, and it is definitely disrespectful of the final sacrifice these pilots have made.

**M14TCN5 Portable Data Reader Unit**

**CS
TIGER
CLAW**
*Executive
Office*
**Commander
Paul Gerald,
2654.02**

## BI-ANNUAL PILOT EVALUATION

## Lt. Rosalind Forbes (callsign Sassy)

### PERFORMANCE

Lt. Forbes is one of the best pilots, possibly the best pilot, aboard the Tiger Claw. She constantly pushes herself to her limits, developing her abilities far faster than regulation sim work and combat drills would permit. Under Lt. Commander Deveraux's guidance, she has learned the technical aspects of her limitations, and no longer seeks to coax more out of her fighter than it can possibly give her. She has not learned restraint, but at least she has learned what is impossible.

In fact, except for the sim fighter contests, she no longer uses the sim as a practice device. I do not think it an exaggeration to say that she has surpassed what the sim can teach. Recently, Lt. Commander Deveraux has been training her personally, taking her out and showing her the intricacies of teamwork under battle conditions. Her skills have improved markedly, and on more than one occasion she has single-handedly pulled victory from a losing situation.

Her most notable accomplishment in the last six months has been a three-kill mission, where her wing was outnumbered three to one.

### LEADERSHIP

Lt. Forbes is very popular with her teammates. Cross-evaluations show that she is regarded as generous and trustworthy.

Her gregarious nature and charisma make her a figure that other pilots automatically look to for direction. She has proven to be a popular wing leader. I believe Lt. Forbes has a definite future in command, assuming her attitude continues to mature.

From my own observation, those she has flown with seek to emulate her "flashy" method of flying, often to the point that they damage their craft. When this was pointed out to her, she temporarily flew more conservatively, but then went back to her own unique style. However, she does seem to be encouraging new pilots to learn the basics before trying stunts, and we'll see if this compromise works out.

### ACTION POINTS

Lt. Forbes should be given more command responsibilities, as they become available.

She should be encouraged to take the appropriate courses, in preparation for advancement.

SCREEN 1 | query "lt st john, cs tiger claw" media=archives/confid
level=CONFIDENTIAL | source=CS Tiger Claw bi-annual pilot eval

**CS TIGER CLAW**
*Executive Office*
**Commander Paul Gerald, 2654.02**

## BI-ANNUAL PILOT EVALUATION

### Lt. Ian St. John (callsign Hunter)

### PERFORMANCE

Lt. St. John is an above-average pilot who has modest natural ability offset by a truly phenomenal determination. He spends hours in the simulator, practicing maneuvers, honing his reflexes and improving his speed. He seems to thrive under Lt. Deveraux's command style, responding with equal determination to both praise and constructive criticism.

His response time, however, seems to have reached its maximum limits. That is to say, his best remains unpromisingly slow. He is aware of the problem and has found an interesting way of compensating for it. Hunter sometimes avoids situations that look like they will turn into dogfights, and instead holds back to support his flight from a distance. This method of lying in wait is somewhat unusual, and definitely not regulation behavior for either a wing leader or wingman, but so far it seems to work. His wingmen say they can depend on his cover fire when they need it.

### LEADERSHIP

Hunter is not a natural leader, although he can be a supportive peer.

He is quickly swayed by the opinions of his peers, is standoffish to people he has not known long, and can be scathing in his opinions of his comrades. His sense of humor is rudimentary, he has difficulty recognizing sarcasm, and he has a history of picking fights with colleagues he feels are laughing at him. It is worth mentioning that since he has started pushing his flying abilities to their limits, he has become less belligerent.

As his abilities and self-confidence improve, he may have time to work on his interpersonal skills, but until then he will remain unsuited to command assignment.

### ACTION POINTS

Lt. St. John should have a complete physical to determine if his reflexes are slow due to medical reasons.

Lt. St. John should, once he achieves his A-class rating, be urged to take CDI training; Interpersonal Conflict Resolutions and Anger Management, in particular.

**M14TCN5 Portable Data Reader Unit**

**CS TIGER CLAW**
*Executive Office*
**Commander Paul Gerald, 2654.02**

## BI-ANNUAL PILOT EVALUATION

## Lt. Adam Polanski (callsign Bishop)

### PERFORMANCE

Lt. Polanski is a skilled front-line pilot, with experience on several carriers and with several varieties of fighters. He is an equally competent wingman and wing leader, able to calmly give or receive orders under fire.

Of particular value is his ability to design and implement battle tactics based on visual, scanner and command-ship communication. He has a firm grasp of how Kilrathi react to different situations, and has on one notable occasion turned the tide from failure to victory, based solely on heat-of-battle calculations.

On another occasion, he was able to lead five pilots in a controlled retreat, bringing them in safely from an asteroid-field ambush. Decoration for this action is pending.

### LEADERSHIP

Although he has only been on the Tiger Claw for three months, I have had to change my opinion of Lt. Polanski several times already. At first he seemed too open and optimistic, and I was concerned that he would not be up to the daily tragedies of front-line battle. It then turned out that was a temporary front, brought on by the stresses of adapting to several new environments in succession. He is in fact a quiet man, inclined to introspection.

His peers respect him, but do not yet feel they know him.

All in all, he is an excellent officer, and could go in any direction that interests him, subject to the needs of the service. My personal suggestion would be Command and Control, although he would also be an excellent flight officer or trainer.

### ACTION POINTS

He should decide what direction he would like his career to proceed, and be given responsibilities in light of that decision.

He should be assigned the position of wing commander as often as feasible, and encouraged to debrief after each mission with a eye to the overall war effort.

SCREEN 1 | query "lt kuhmelo, cs tiger claw" media=archives/confid
level=CONFIDENTIAL | source=CS Tiger Claw bi-annual pilot eval

**CS TIGER CLAW**
*Executive Office*
**Commander Paul Gerald, 2654.02**

## BI-ANNUAL PILOT EVALUATION

## Lt. Joseph Kuhmelo (callsign Knight)

### PERFORMANCE

Lt. Kuhmelo's ability as a fighter pilot is actually much greater than would appear from his kill score or personal goal success. Statistically, he looks to be one of our poorer pilots, but in fact, I'd be inclined to argue the opposite.

I have been made aware that a great deal of his time in the cockpit is spent "coaching" the raw pilots. He has talked at least two pilots through their first kills, and that could not be done by someone who does not have a thorough understanding of both his ship and his enemy.

He has among the highest scores in the sim, and is a popular partner in the team exercises.

His low kill score could be due to "giving" his kills away, but actually I am more concerned that he may be hesitating to kill for personal or philosophical reasons.

He has a personal affinity for bombing missions, and is currently at the top of the Broadsword flight roster.

### LEADERSHIP

Knight is well-liked by his peers, respected by his superiors, and known by name to most of the other divisions of the ship. His opinions are given full consideration, and he readily accepts the advice of others. He admits when he is wrong, and does not seem to hold grudges against anyone he works with.

He has been known to "herd" panicked pilots back to base, during times of radio silence. He has a deep concern for wingmen who are in over their heads.

Once again, my only concern is his low kill score. If he does not fully support the war effort, he obviously cannot be promoted beyond his current status. Any doubts that continue to exist may begin to fester, at which point it would be dangerous to entrust him with command decisions.

### ACTION POINTS

Lt. Kuhmelo should be encouraged to continue training new pilots.

He should talk to a ship's counselor to discover if there are any pre-set prejudices against combat or the role of a fighter pilot.

**M14TCN5 Portable Data Reader Unit**

# M *Marine Boarding Protocol*

**462** ▮▮ CONFED MARINE CORPS SOP DOCUMENT ▮▮

### DEFINITIONS

A *boarding operation* is an operation wherein a boarding party is inserted into a vessel known or suspected to be under enemy control, with an objective of securing or sabotaging said vessel.

A *boarding party* is a combat detail (consisting of one or more boarding squads) assigned to carry out a boarding operation.

A *boarding squad* is an operational unit consisting of three to five armored fire teams plus one OIC and one Hospital Corpsman.

A *fire team* is a team of two armored marines.

The *OIC (officer in charge)* is an officer or senior NCO assigned command authority over a boarding squad.

### PROCEDURES

A boarding operation must be declared by the captain of a ship-in-space, or the base commander of a permanent installation. The captain/commander will then appoint a Marine, Naval or Space Force officer as Mission Commander for the operation. The Mission Commander shall be responsible for tactical coordination of the operation, to include selection of forces and assignment and prioritization of mission objectives. All decisions by the Mission Commander are subject to review and approval by the ship's captain/base commander.

The Mission Commander may serve as OIC of a boarding squad, or may coordinate the operation from a tactical command center (usually located at or near the point of ingress into the vessel being boarded). The former option is most appropriate to small operations, while the latter is preferable for very large-scale operations. ──────────

**SCREEN 2** | query "boarding protocol, confed marines"
**level=CONFIDENTIAL** | source=confed marine corps.sop.m–462.document

Where possible, a heavy demolition team should be held in reserve to support the boarding party as needed (see *SOP Doc. M-531, Shipboard Demolition Operations*). Heavy demo teams may facilitate ingress through strong structural barriers, and may also be instrumental in the sabotage or destruction of the boarded vessel, if those goals are part of the mission plan.

In missions where control of the enemy vessel is an objective, a prize crew (selected by the captain/base commander) should be held in reserve.

Boarding parties may enter the enemy ship from a friendly cap ship, troop transport shuttle or other delivery craft. The commander of this delivery craft shall have full authority at any time to disengage from the enemy ship, should the tactical situation make it prudent to do so. This discretionary authority exists independent of whether the boarding party has been successfully recovered from the enemy vessel.

All combat operations shall be conducted by Marine fire teams in accordance with the procedures outlined in *SOP Doc. M-121, Shipboard Tactical Combat.*

*The following priorities are recommended for boarding operations designed to establish control of an enemy vessel.*

1. Secure the bridge(s).
2. Secure the engine room(s).
3. Secure all weapons control areas.
4. Neutralize any remaining enemy resistance.

**M14TCN5 Portable Data Reader Unit**

# Standard Issue Equipment for Boarding Parties

### C-524 Space Armor

C-524 Space Armor consists of a pressure suit molded from rubberized plastic reinforced with monofilament polymers. The interior of the suit houses a life-support system providing for air recirculation, temperature regulation and insulation, radiation shielding, and bodily waste elimination and storage. The exterior of the suit is bonded to polymer armor plates protecting primary target areas.

Space Armor is a single-piece unit that is donned via an aperture on the left side, extending from hip to neck. This aperture is protected with a double-sealed molecular bonding strip controlled by a stud on the interior collar of the suit. For added safety, the C-512 Combat Helmet cannot be attached to the suit until the suit is sealed, and the seal cannot be released until the helmet is removed.

The suit (including all plates and life-support equipment) weighs 2.4 kg, and can be folded for storage into a self-contained pouch measuring 29 x 24 x 14 cm. Two sealable, external thigh-pockets are provided for small item storage, and a pouch below the right arm contains a standard emergency patch kit. Additional capacity for equipment or armaments may be mounted to a C-545 External Web Harness (optional for boarding parties).

## C-532 Life Support Pack

The C-532 Life Support Pack is a sealed, integrated unit designed to support human life under combat conditions for up to seven hours. It incorporates a seven-hour air supply (six-hour regular tank plus one-hour ancillary emergency tank) with circulation fans, a one-quart water tank, heater/coolant unit and 72-hour power supply. The entire unit is protected by a half inch of polymer armor overall.

The climate-control system is rated for continuous operation from -43 to 98 degrees centigrade (used in conjunction with undamaged C-524 Space Armor & C-512 Combat Helmet).

The C-532 connects to the C-512 Combat Helmet via an umbilicus hose of monofilament-reinforced plastic, and to the C-524 Space Armor via direct mount. Either connection is sufficient to sustain life support (although strenuous activity is not recommended if only the direct mount linkage is in use, as oxygen deprivation can result). There is also a recessed emergency umbilicus stored in an armored compartment behind the right shoulder, which can be deployed if the primary umbilicus is damaged, or to allow a second individual to use the same C-532 unit under emergency conditions.

Connectors for the air tanks, water tanks and power supply recharge are located in a sealed, armored compartment at the unit's base. All three operations can be conducted while the unit is in use, given access to appropriate pumping/charging equipment.

Weight (with full air and water tanks) 8.4 kg. Dimensions 41 x 32 x 20 cm.

**M14TCN5 Portable Data Reader Unit**

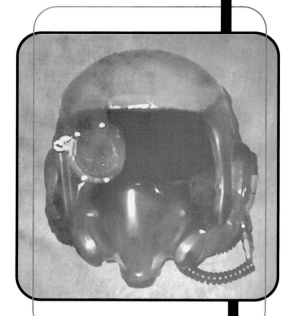

## C-512 Combat Helmet

The C-512 Combat Helmet is an integrated imaging/communications/life support/protective unit. The basic shell is a 3 cm thickness of polymer armor, including the visor, which is a fiber-optically clarified polymer. It is fully insulated and shielded. The fiberoptic visor provides automatic glare and flash protection, plus infrared imaging and light-enhancement options. It can also generate up to two floating HUDs capable of displaying text or schematics. Visor underlighting is provided for illumination.

Its voice-activated, 40-channel communications system with integral antenna is rated for a range of up to 8000 kilometers across open space.

A water nipple is accessible to the right of the visor, and a pill dispenser capable of dispensing pain-killers, stimulants, anti-rad or anti-agent medications is accessible to the left.

A micro-processor is capable of slotting up to four data, targeting or navigation cards. The unit is powered with a rechargeable power cell rated for 48 hours continuous operation at maximum output.

Weight 4.3 kg. Dimensions 35 x 33 x 30 cm.

## C-47 Assault Rifle

The standard assault weapon of all ship-based Confed forces, the C-47 Assault Rifle incorporates a ballistic rifle and an underslung grenade launcher. The rifle fires an explosive 2.3 mm caseless projectile along a tight-beam magnetic field. The grenade launcher fires magnetically accelerated 3.5 cm concussion micro-grenades.

**SCREEN 6** | query "boarding protocol, confed marines"
level=CONFIDENTIAL | source=confed marine corps.sop.m–462.document

As a rifle, the C-47 can be set to single fire, three- or five-round burst fire, or fully automatic fire. (The grenade launcher is single-shot only.)

A dual-feed magazine holds 100 projectiles and 20 micro-grenades. (An optional banana-clip magazine can hold 175 projectiles and 30 micro-grenades.) The magnetic accelerator is powered with a sealed rechargeable power cell mounted in the butt, rated for 25,000 individual firings.

The C-47 should be carried by all fire-team members in boarding operations. Officers may carry the C-47 or the C-244 Pistol.

Weight (fully loaded, standard clip) 5.1 kg. Dimensions 88 cm x 21 cm x 7 cm.

## C-244 Pistol

The C-244 Pistol is the standard shipboard sidearm for Confed forces. It fires an explosive 2.3 mm caseless projectile along a tight-beam magnetic field. It can be set to fire single shots or 3-round bursts.

Clips are mounted in the grip, and have a capacity of 100 rounds. The magnetic accelerator is powered with a sealed rechargeable

power cell rated for 25,000 individual firings. The power cell is mounted in the grip, above the ammo bay.

On boarding operations it should be carried by all medics, and may be carried by officers in lieu of the C-47.

Weight (fully loaded) 1.7 kg. Dimensions 19 cm x 11 cm x 6 cm.

**M14TCN5 Portable Data Reader Unit**

## C-275 Utility Knife (Not Shown)

The C-275 Utility Knife is a beryllium-carbon alloy blade mounted into a hardened stenplas handle. The handle has a shaped grip for combat with a stenplas handguard, and the knife is balanced for throwing. In addition to combat use, the C-275 has number of utility uses (for digging or scraping, or use as a wedge or lever). A titanium strike plate mounted on the end of the handle allows it to be used as a striking surface. The C-275 should be carried by all members of a boarding party, including fire teams, medics, and officers.

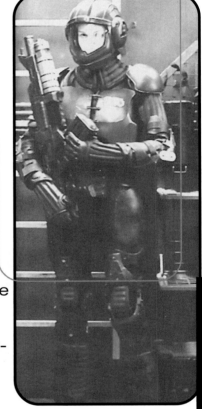

Weight .8 kg. Dimensions 40 x 6 x 2 cm.

## C-643 Shaped Satchel Charge (Not Shown)

The C-643 Shaped Satchel Charge is a self-adhesive, shaped, timed explosive device. It is designed to blow hatches and other light barriers, but may also be used against personnel. The C-643's timer may be set for a 5- to 60-second delay. A back-up timer has a fixed 10-second delay, and may also be used with a trip-wire trigger—when the trip-wire is set, the 10-second delay is activated, and at the end of that time any further disturbance to the trigger will ignite the device.

Due to the shaping of the explosive force, personnel may safely remain as close as 5 meters to the rear of a C-643 explosion. However, a distance of at least 25 meters is recommended, due to the possibility of ancillary damage and debris.

One C-643 should be carried by each fire team not already carrying a C-884.

Weight .8 kg. Dimensions 12 x 12 x 5 cm.

## C-884 MEDIUM CUTTING TORCH (NOT SHOWN)

The C-884 Medium Cutting Torch is a tripod-mounted laser cutting torch designed for cutting through non-reinforced bulkheads and airlocks. In emergencies, the C-884 can be used as a short-range anti-personnel weapon. The C-884 has a structural cutting range of 2 meters, and an offensive range of about 7 meters. The tripod mount is adjustable in height, from .1 meter to 1.6 meters above the deck. The unit is powered by a sealed, rechargeable power cell, and can sustain up to 1 hour of continuous operation.

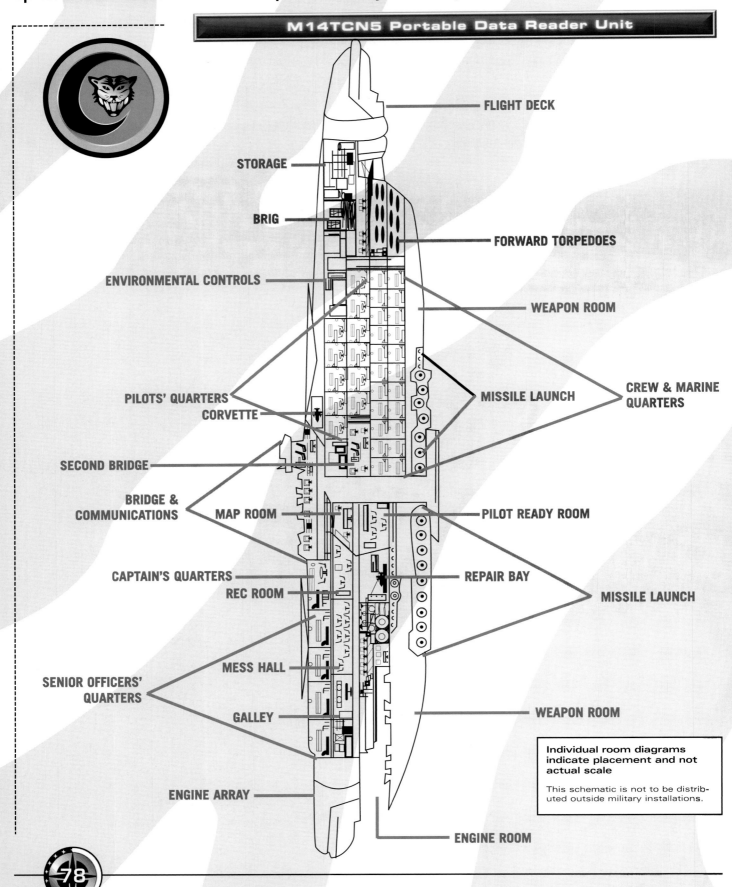

**M14TCN5 Portable Data Reader Unit**

FLIGHT DECK

STORAGE

BRIG

FORWARD TORPEDOES

ENVIRONMENTAL CONTROLS

WEAPON ROOM

PILOTS' QUARTERS

CORVETTE

MISSILE LAUNCH

CREW & MARINE QUARTERS

SECOND BRIDGE

BRIDGE & COMMUNICATIONS

MAP ROOM

PILOT READY ROOM

CAPTAIN'S QUARTERS

REPAIR BAY

REC ROOM

MISSILE LAUNCH

SENIOR OFFICERS' QUARTERS

MESS HALL

GALLEY

WEAPON ROOM

ENGINE ARRAY

Individual room diagrams indicate placement and not actual scale

This schematic is not to be distributed outside military installations.

ENGINE ROOM

**SCREEN 2** | query "deck plans, cs tiger claw" level=**CONFIDENTIAL**
source=csn.ship in service.schematics.tigerclaw

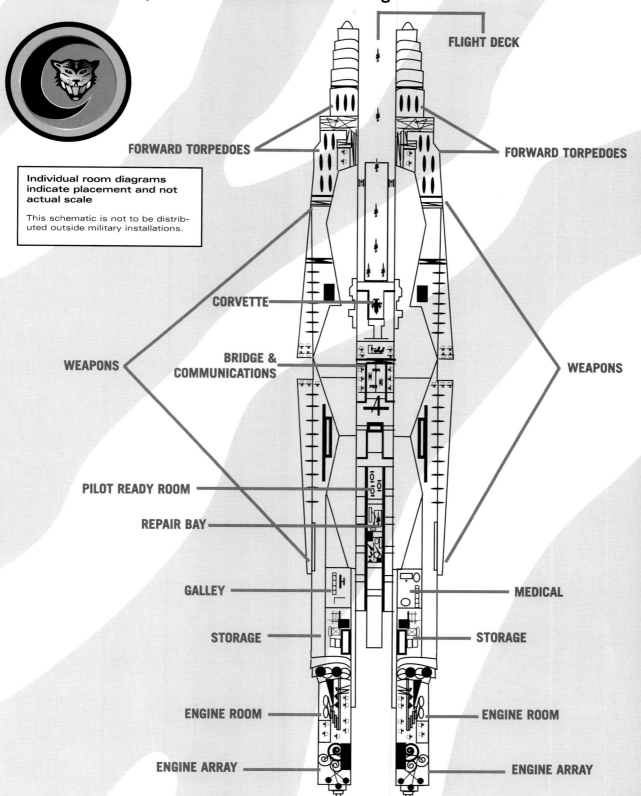

FLIGHT DECK

FORWARD TORPEDOES

FORWARD TORPEDOES

> Individual room diagrams
> indicate placement and not
> actual scale
>
> This schematic is not to be distrib-
> uted outside military installations.

CORVETTE

WEAPONS

BRIDGE &
COMMUNICATIONS

WEAPONS

PILOT READY ROOM

REPAIR BAY

GALLEY

MEDICAL

STORAGE

STORAGE

ENGINE ROOM

ENGINE ROOM

ENGINE ARRAY

ENGINE ARRAY

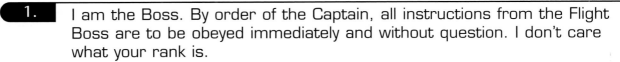

# FLIGHT DECK PROTOCOL, CS TIGER CLAW

**MCPO G. Peterson, Deck Boss**

**The following instructions apply to all personnel on the Flight Deck. If you don't understand these rules, do not enter the deck.**

1. I am the Boss. By order of the Captain, all instructions from the Flight Boss are to be obeyed immediately and without question. I don't care what your rank is.

2. During normal operations, all instructions from the Flight Control Officer on duty are to be followed immediately and without question. Only the Deck Boss can override instructions from the FCO. During emergency situations, all instructions from the Emergency Crew Chief are to be followed immediately and without question. Only the Deck Boss can override instructions from the ECC during emergency situations.

3. All personnel working the deck will wear either a utility coverall or a flight suit. Pilots will do no maintenance on their craft in flight suits, except for pre-flight checklists.

4. Absolutely no one on deck during scrambles except on-duty pilots and deck crew. If you think you have business on deck during a scramble, report to control bay first. No exceptions!

5. No horseplay on the deck, no loitering on the deck. If you're not working, get out!

6. All personnel will make way for utility tractor and fuel bowser at all times.

7. Diagnostics on craft engines and weapons systems that require a hot start-up will only be conducted with the express permission of the Deck Boss, under the personal supervision of the Deck Boss, Propulsion Chief, or Weapon System Chief.

8. No craft will launch or land from this deck without personal authorization from the Flight Control Officer.

9. No food or drink on the flight deck. If you're on break, go to the galley for your snack.

## SCREEN 2 | query "flight deck protocol, confed naval"
source=mil.archive.pers.cn.tigerclaw.MCPO.9842-68399

**10.** Pilots and techs ONLY in cockpits. Guests must have permission of the Captain and the Deck Boss before entering or viewing a cockpit, and must be personally escorted by a pilot at all times while on deck.

**11.** No craft will launch from this deck until a pre-flight checklist is complete. If the Captain declares a flush scramble, abbreviated checklists may be used. Full checklists WILL be used at ALL OTHER times.

**12.** ENVIRONMENTAL MAINTENANCE FIELD: NOBODY crosses the red line except launching/landing craft and field maintenance crews. Field crews will undertake hot operations only at the express orders of the Deck Boss.

**13.** EMERGENCY OPERATIONS: If the emergency klaxon sounds, all other deck traffic will yield to repair and medical crews, IN THAT ORDER.

**14.** If the breech klaxon sounds, all personnel will immediately go to the life-support lockers and don environmental gear.

**15.** Any pilot or crewman may sound the emergency klaxon at any time. I'd rather have the klaxon go when there is no emergency, than have it not go when there is one. HOWEVER, any bogus or prank alarms will be referred directly to Captain's Mast.

**16.** NO HOT LANDINGS! All craft will approach the deck with engines and primary maneuvering thrusters off. Only landing thrusters will be used for attitude correction.

**17.** Exterior deck. No craft will launch or land unless the exterior deck is 100% clear. This includes craft, debris, utility tractor, or personnel.

**18.** All wreckage will be cleared from the exterior deck immediately. Rescue operations will be coordinated by the FCO once the deck is clear.

**19.** Except in the case of medical emergency or express orders from the Captain, no pilot will leave the deck until your craft is berthed, secured, and pre-prepped.

**20.** No one except the Deck Boss can authorize any transfer of parts from one craft to another.

**21.** If a craft is redlined, it will be removed from the flight deck immediately. Redline craft will remain in the repair bay until certified ready for space.

**M14TCN5 Portable Data Reader Unit**

# *Semi-Annual Report to Confederation Headquarters Detailing Casualties Among the 88th Fighter Wing Assigned to CS Tiger Claw*

## Covering the Period 2653.246—2654.075

Lieutenant Kendal "Cueball" Kendrick, 2653.264
*killed in action against the Kilrathi enemy*

Lieutenant JG Amhar "Dragster" Bagheer, 2653.270
*killed in action against the Kilrathi enemy*

Lieutenant Roosevelt "Motown" Sullivan, 2653.282
*killed in action against the Kilrathi enemy*

Lieutenant Camilla "Grinder" Saint James, 2653.292
*Her Rapier already badly damaged, and her wingman, Lt. Krishu, a casualty, Lt. Saint James verbally challenged and then engaged over a dozen of the Kilrathi enemy, allowing the other wing of her flight, which also had sustained severe damage, to return safely to the Tiger Claw. For bravely sacrificing her own life that others might survive, it is recommended that Lt. Saint James be awarded the Bronze Star.*

Lieutenant JG Prem "Capulet" Krishu, 2653.292
*killed in action against the Kilrathi enemy*

Lieutenant Hermione "Kilroy" Alexander, 2653.296
*killed in action against the Kilrathi enemy*

Lieutenant Commander Harlan "Fat Lady" Elliott, 2653.299
*killed in action against the Kilrathi enemy*

Lieutenant JG Scala "Ratbert" Scotia, 2653.299
*killed in action against the Kilrathi enemy*

Lieutenant Constantine "Kinkajou" Andropolous, 2653.306
*killed in action against the Kilrathi enemy*

Lieutenant Samhain "Kinko" Samuell, 2653.307
*killed in action against the Kilrathi enemy*

Lieutenant JG Clarence "Phoenix" McCloud, 2653.309
*killed in action against the Kilrathi enemy*

Lieutenant Daoud "Fabian" People, 2653.309
*killed in action against the Kilrathi enemy*

Lieutenant Commander Lilly "Catnip" Belle, 2653.309
*killed in action against the Kilrathi enemy*

Lieutenant JG Farrell "Ralph" Malph, 2653.312
*killed in action against the Kilrathi enemy*

Lieutenant Xiou "Shushu" Wilson, 2653.312
*killed in action against the Kilrathi enemy*

Lieutenant Gabriella "Axxialla" Carpentinu, 2653.315
*killed in action against the Kilrathi enemy*

Lieutenant JG Edmund "Streaker" Warbarch, 2653.365

Lieutenant Commander Helen "Cassiopeia" Condon, 2653.365

Lieutenant Sinjean "Schlitterbahn" Brun, 2653.365

Lieutenant JG Serene "Witch Hazel" Sandalabra, 2653.365

Lieutenant Melanie "Topdog" Maxwell, 2654.001
*Undertaking a recon in force, Lt. Cmdr. Condon commanded a flight to investigate sensor anomalies near Cairo III. Ambushed by a full squadron of enemy fighter craft, her flight acquitted itself in exemplary manner, recording 23 confirmed kills and 5 probable kills. By springing this ambush prematurely, and then effectively neutralizing it, Lt. Condon's flight prevented the Tiger Claw from entering harm's way. Only Lt. Maxwell and Lt. Polanski survived this encounter, and regretably, Lt. Maxwell died the next day of wounds sustained in this action. In this action alone, Lt. Warbach qualified as an Ace, while Lt. Cmdr. Condon achieved Ace of Ace standing.*

*For meritorious conduct in confronting the Kilrathi enemy, it is recommended that Lts. Warbach, Brun, Sandalabra, Maxwell, and Polanski be awarded the Silver Star, and Lt. Cmdr. Condon the Gold Star.*

Lieutenant JG Wim "Excelsior" Campesi, 2654.042
*killed in action against the Kilrathi enemy*

Lieutenant JG BJ "Bubba" Wilamett, 2654.042
*killed in action against the Kilrathi enemy*

Lieutenant Chakra "Shiva" Yanklip, 2654.045
*killed in action against the Kilrathi enemy*

Lieutenant JG William "Carnival" Jefferson, 2654.070
*killed in action against the Kilrathi enemy*

Lieutenant Commander Chen "Bossman" Kien, 2654.070
*After successfully leading his flight against a Kilrathi corvette and escort, Lt. Cmdr. Kien delayed his own safe return in order to shepherd his damaged wingman, Lt. Jefferson. Encountering superior enemy numbers, Lt. Cmdr. Kien fought bravely, but was eventually overwhelmed.*

*For valor in the face of the enemy, and for risking his own welfare for the sake of a comrade, it is recommended that Lt. Cmdr. Kien be awarded his second Bronze Star.*

# COMMON CONFEDERATION AND KILRATHI SHIPS
# RELATIVE SIZE AND SILHOUETTE RECOGNITION CHART

This chart should be made available to all sen/com operators, flight crews, and other relevant personnel pursuant to section 5847-23 of the Dash 866 Onboard Ops manual.

**Snakeir-Class Super-Dreadnought**
915m

**Concordia-Class Supercruiser**
855m

**Sivar-Class Dreadnought**
825m

**Bengal-Class Strike Carrier**
625m

**Fralthi-Class Cruiser**
475m

**Ralari-Class Destroyer**
385m

**Typical Civilian Merchant (Light Cargo)**
25m

(Specs and silhouette are Proxima Spaceworks' Errant model.)

**CF-131 Broadsword**
12m

**CF-117b Rapier**
9m

**KF-100 Dralthi**
9m

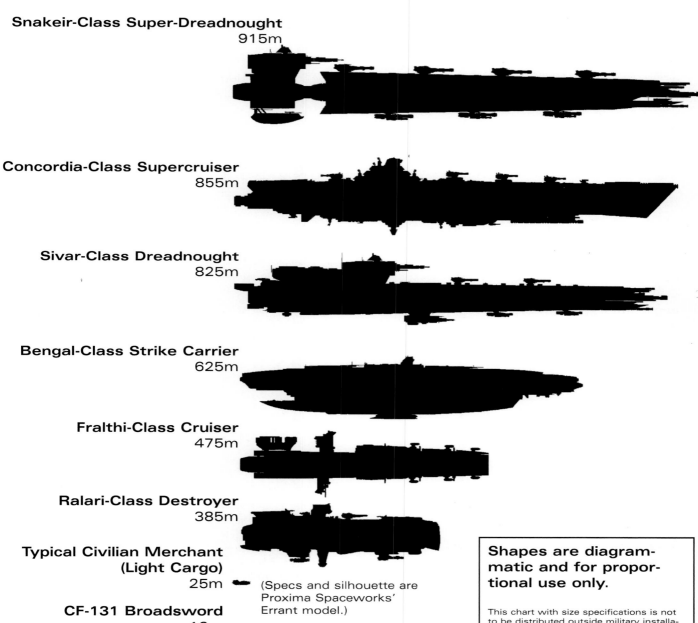

**Shapes are diagrammatic and for proportional use only.**

This chart with size specifications is not to be distributed outside military installations. Copies without this information are available for *Shipwatch!* and corollary programs from Civilian Action League offices.

**M14TCN5 Portable Data Reader Unit**

# KILRATHI TACTICS

**Document C776b-12, #12 in a series, published by the Office of Tactical Intelligence**

In planning effective offensive and defensive operations against the Kilrathi, it is first necessary to understand the underlying principles that guide Kilrathi tactical decisions. And before those principles can be understood, it is necessary to understand how the Kilrathi mind works.

Kilrathi are not human beings and do not think or react like human beings. The presuppositions behind their tactical philosophy are rooted in their racial evolution.

Before discussing the presuppositions of Kilrathi tactics, a vital distinction must be drawn. Kilrathi are neither animals nor machines. They are highly intelligent, adaptable and self-aware sentients. The Kilrathi understand the patterns of their thought processes better than we ever can, and they are fully capable of designing and carrying out tactics that specifically avoid their normal patterns of behavior.

Understanding the patterns of Kilrathi tactical assumptions can be an invaluable tool, particularly in large-scale or impromptu actions, but it can be a fatal error to assume that the Kilrathi will *always* behave according to these patterns.

The Kilrathi are descended from predators—pack-hunters. Humans are also descended from predators, but our ancestors were hunter-gatherers. Early Kilrathi ancestors reached the top of the food chain much quicker than proto-humans did.

Kilrathi are naturally predisposed to attack over defense, and to ambush over attack-in-force. They are natural guerrilla fighters.

Proto-Kilrathi hunting packs would conceal themselves along known game-trails, lie in wait until a herd of food-animals passed by, identify the weakest, most vulnerable prey, and execute a coordinated attack. Early humans also used similar tactics, of course, but not until they achieved sentience and began to make weapons—three or four million years ago. Kilrathi have been hunting in this fashion, using instinct and natural weaponry, for at least 10 million years.

This means that pack-hunting tactics are very deeply ingrained in the Kilrathi psyche. Again, anything the Kilrathi instinct suggests, the Kilrathi intellect can overrule, but the pack-hunter paradigm is the one that comes the most naturally to the Kilrathi, and therefore the one they will turn to under stress, or when they believe they have the advantage.

Some general principles are implied by the evolutionary psychology of the Kilrathi. These general principles are supported by the majority of current after-battle debriefings.

*Kilrathi are most comfortable attacking in groups.* In groups of three or more, Kilrathi warriors will often display suicidal courage, and engage numerically superior forces. However, a lone Kilrathi (and sometimes a pair) will tend to avoid contact, even against an evenly matched enemy.

*Kilrathi have a natural affinity for the ambush.* A lone Kilrathi is frequently a decoy planted to lure opposing forces into an ambush situation.

*Kilrathi will sometimes fixate on a wounded enemy*, pursuing it to the death, while ignoring more dangerous, undamaged opponents. This happens enough that Confed tacticians have given it a name . . . it is called a "blood frenzy."

Because of their affinity for group tactics, Kilrathi are not naturally prone to sabotage or spy operations involving the insertion and action of a single operative.

The Kilrathi are, of course, fully aware of these tendencies in their psyche—they have been exploiting them against each other in inter-clan warfare for millennia. As a race, they have developed numerous social constructs designed to bypass these racial tendencies when it is advantageous to do so. However, these social constructs, in turn, also represent trends in Kilrathi behavior which can be successfully exploited in battle if fully understood.

These behaviors include:

- Obey without question

- Focus on the strongest

- Respond to challenge

**M14TCN5 Portable Data Reader Unit**

## Obey without question

This is the most basic and pervasive social tenet of Kilrathi martial culture. Imagination and creativity are only encouraged in senior commanders and nobles. Line troops are trained to simply follow orders, specifically and without question or interpretation. The conceptual basis for this custom, it is believed, is the idea that a warrior given specific instructions can concentrate on fulfilling them, to the exclusion of other distractions, while a warrior given more general goals may become distracted by instinctive hunting behaviors, to the detriment of the overall strategic mission. The advantage to be seized here by the enemies of the Kilrathi is that if the opposing force can successfully make the Kilrathi mission goals unachievable or logically impossible, the Kilrathi force will sometimes be thrown into complete chaos, particularly if not under the direct supervision of a dominant leader.

## Focus on the strongest

The Kilrathi hunting instinct to run down the weakest opponent has been thoroughly discussed. The strategic inappropriateness of such behavior in warfare—leaving the strongest and most dangerous members of the opposing force free to react, while focusing on the weakest—was obvious to the Kilrathi from the very earliest period of their social development. The solution was a custom that has become one of the central principles of all Kilrathi tactics—focus an attack on the enemy's strongest asset first. This tendency can be exploited if the Kilrathi can be deceived about where the strongest asset of an opposing force actually lies. Another potentially viable tactic can involve putting the strongest asset in the forefront of the battle, in a strong defensive posture, allowing the remainder of the force to execute a coordinated attack on the flanks while the Kilrathi forces are focused on overcoming the primary target's defenses.

"... I serve my Hrai and Lord
With my tongue I offer fealty
With my claws I unsheathe victory."

*— From a Kilrathi oath*

*Wording in these oaths varies from clan to clan, but the theme of unquestioning obedience remains constant.*

**"My claws do not know shame
For I am a warrior of Kilrah . . .
And offer up my life for honor."**

*Recovered Kilrathi writings, both military and non-military, reference honor and shame, often linked with combat to the death. The shame/honor dichotomy is thus made central to Kilrathi martial philosophy.*

## Respond to challenge

A Kilrathi warrior must answer a challenge to combat. Reasonable precautions may be taken to ensure that a challenge is not a veiled trap, but in general any challenge or insult is grounds for a struggle to the death. Such behavior is not only legal and accepted in the Kilrathi military, it is in fact punishable by death for a warrior to back down from single combat. It is theorized that presentient Kilrathi displayed dominance patterns typical of pack-hunters, whereby a smaller or inferior hunter would respond with submissive displays to any challenge from a dominant pack-leader. This dominance/submission behavior still underlies many Kilrathi institutions, from the Imperial Throne on down, but it is not tenable in a warfare context, where it may be necessary for lesser warriors to engage obviously more potent enemies. Therefore, Kilrathi are conditioned to respond violently to any challenge to their prowess or honor. (This general rule is greatly complicated in the specific case of Kilrathi commanders and their subordinates. However, the very complex codes that govern challenge/submission behavior between commanders and inferiors is not germane to this discussion.) This conditioning can be exploited in battle through the use of verbal taunts (under conditions where interspecies communication is possible) or by displays of reckless courage. Such behaviors can sometimes distract members of a Kilrathi force from their primary objectives. (There is, of course, significant risk to the challenger in most such situations.)

**M14TCN5 Portable Data Reader Unit**

## Space Tactics

Kilrathi naval strategy tends to view capital ships as more defensive than offensive assets, and as more strategic than tactical in function. The bulk of the offensive effort in a Kilrathi naval engagement is carried by fighters and fighter-bombers. Cap ships are used as staging platforms, or for long-range missile bombardment of planetary targets, permanent space stations and opposing cap ships.

If assaulted by a task force of opposing cap ships, a Kilrathi ship usually tries to withdraw under cover of its own guns and scrambled escort fighters. Most Kilrathi battleships larger than a destroyer incorporate a hangar and carrier deck from which escort fighters may be scrambled. Kilrathi battleships almost never engage in a pitched gun- or torpedo-battle with an equivalent opposing force.

The exception to the above is the Kilrathi destroyer, which (much like its Confed counterpart) is a small, heavily armed battleship with no carrier capacity. Destroyers are used for fleet defense—they provide screening actions for the carriers in a battle group, to prevent opposing forces from making direct assaults on the strategically vital carrier decks.

In fighter combat, the Kilrathi are at their most dangerous. They use the same tactics in space that their hunter ancestors used against larger, faster prey in the primordial past. The Kilrathi tend to attack in tight formations (which can make them vulnerable to guided missile barrages launched early in the engagement), surrounding and overwhelming their opponents. They will often make use of decoys, sending one fighter out to engage the enemy one-on-one, then assume a defensive posture, hoping the enemy will chase it while two, three or more fighters get on the pursuer's six.

Kilrathi fighters are optimized for speed and maneuverability, and can be almost impossible to run down if they go purely on the defensive. In such situations, if simple marksmanship fails, the Kilrathi defender should be engaged with a guided missile, or

caught in a crossfire. Sometimes the evading Kilrathi can be taunted into going on the offensive, if the attacker has a sufficient command of Kilrathi psychology.

All Kilrathi warriors are trained as both soldiers and pilots, but only the best pilots are actually assigned to fighters. Kilrathi honor their elite fighter pilots even more than Confed honors its Aces, and a particularly notable Kilrathi hero will often be given a personalized fighter by the leader of their clan, with individualized markings and (often) technical innovations designed to optimize the Ace's fighting style. Any Kilrathi fighter with anomalous markings, particularly if behaving in a particularly aggressive manor or displaying atypically high performance, should be treated as an extreme threat—Kilrathi Ace status is not bestowed lightly, and those who earn it are genuinely dangerous.

## Boarding Actions

In ship-to-ship boarding actions, Kilrathi tend to enter explosively and advance aggressively. A Kilrathi boarding party consists of about four to 20 small units of four to eight warriors each. Once inside the target ship, the boarding party spreads out as fast as possible throughout the ship, destroying anything that stands in their way. This aggressive offense gives the defenders very little time to adjust to changing conditions, but it can also leave the Kilrathi attackers vulnerable to being cornered or bracketed by alert defensive forces.

In boarding parties, Kilrathi are typically lightly armed, carrying only the Dor-Chak laser rifle and four to six fragmentation grenades. If engaged in hand-to-hand combat, the Kilrathi usually employ their natural claws. Even armed with a knife or staff, humans are grievously overmatched against Kilrathi warriors in close combat. The three-inch Kilrathi claws are capable of cleanly severing a human spinal column, and the average Kilrathi warrior has sufficient strength to dead-lift about 700 kg overhead.

The best tactic against Kilrathi boarders is to isolate the units, cut them off, pin them down and destroy them. Kilrathi units are optimized for offense, not defense, and if they can be immobilized they become much less dangerous.

**M14TCN5 Portable Data Reader Unit**

## Kilrathi Combat Armor

For at least 1000 years before they discovered space flight, the standard Kilrathi military uniform has been a suit of jointed metal plates. Today, except for the materials used, a spacefaring Kilrathi warrior wears the same uniform that his ancestors wore twelve centuries ago.

The basic structure of the armor remains steel plates, although a sophisticated alloy is now used. Also, the plates are coated with a plastic film that disrupts many energy weapons and also offers some protection against hard radiation. A full suit of Kilrathi armor (with helmet) weighs about 45 kg.

The interior of the suit is coated with fiber "hairs" that interlock under life-support conditions to seal off the suit from atmosphere and heat loss. Life support systems are integrated into the suit, and are rudimentary compared to similar human devices. An external breathing supply is not necessary except for protracted missions, as the Kilrathi metabolism and the filtering action of the semi-organic "hairs" allows them to re-breathe the atmosphere within the suit itself for several hours. Under normal circumstances, the only electronic device in a Kilrathi armor suit is the helmet radio, powered by a photonicly charged crystalline power supply.

One unusual feature of Kilrathi armor is that the tips of the fingers are usually kept exposed, to allow the warrior to use his extendible claws in close combat.

The helmet visor is coated with a polarizing agent (very similar to the transparent plastic coating over the armor itself) which provides excellent protection against glare. This is an important consideration, since Kilrathi eyes are optimized for a lower level of light than human.

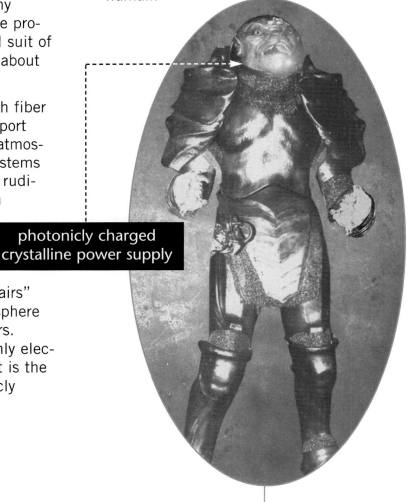

photonicly charged crystalline power supply

### Dor-Chak Laser Rifle

The standard Kilrathi sidearm in shipboard operations is a light energy weapon called the Dor-Chak ("Striking Bird") in the Kilrathi tongue. It usually weighs about 6 kg, and measures 29 cm from barrel-tip to the end of the stock. (Some clans wield variant Dor-Chaks, which may look some-what different from the standard model, but most function virtually identically.) It is believed that the Dor-Chak, in its modern form, was developed by the Kilrathi 50 to 100 years before contact with humanity.

The Dor-Chak is a multifunction weapon. There's a short-range, wide-beam setting (good for about 10 meters against unar-mored targets, with a spread of about 2 meters), a long-range narrow-beam setting

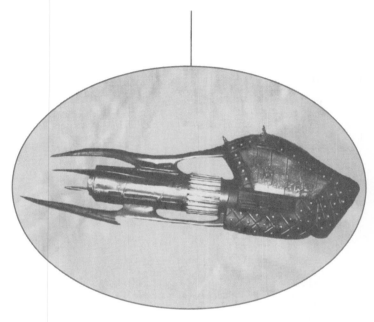

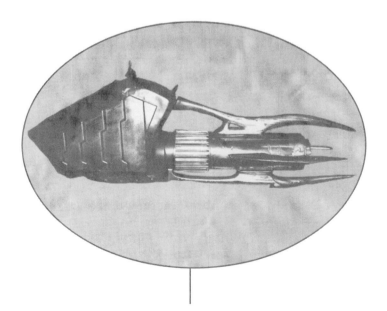

(able to penetrate an unarmored human tar-get at 200 meters), plus a 1-meter torch mode, for cutting through hatches and bulkheads. Its crystalline power supply is good for about 20 minutes of continuous use, after which it must be discarded and a new one slotted into its place. Most Kilrathi warriors go into battle carrying at least five fully charged power supplies for their Dor-Chak.

Confed's M-47 semiautomatic laser, which is quickly becoming the standard weapon for planetary operations, is based directly on technology originally created by the Kilrathi for the Dor-Chak.

**IP Port Status:** undocked    **OP Port Status:** undocked
**Clearance Key Status:** insertcard_verifying_denied_accepted
**Data Security Level:** unclassified_confidential_secret_topsecret

 View  Store  Delete

## PEGASUS NAVAL BASE

Excerpted from the Confed Military Installation Index, 2653 edition.

 View  Store  Delete

## COMMAND OFFICER PROFILES

Not to be opened except with the express written permission of Admiral Tolwyn, or in accordance with the procedures of Sect. D-147 paragraph G . . .

 View  Store  Delete

## CN THREAT REPORT K459-C

Based on intelligence analysis, development by the enemy of the Ultra-Long-Range Phased Photon-Cloak Torpedo, aka "Skipper Missile" . . .

View  Store  Delete

# LOSS OF THE CS *IASON*

At 0450 hours on *2638.229*, *Iason* made visual contact
with three Kilrathi B'ru'k-class merchantmen . . .

query "secret update" media=org_ops, level=SECRET | return=4 . . .
Retrieving 4 text files + graphical subfiles . . .

Your search is being monitored and recorded. Keying search #892S . . .
reference this search code to recall articles.
Please insert data chip . . . You may view, store, or delete.

    article 1 of 4="pegasus naval base"
    article 2 of 4="profile cn senior officers"
    article 3 of 4="kilrathi skipper missile"
    article 4 of 4="loss of iason, inquiry report"

SECRET

**M14TCN5 Portable Data Reader Unit**

# PEGASUS NAVAL BASE

*Excerpted from the Confed Military Installation Index, 2653 edition.*

**Location:** D-5 asteroid belt (Asteroid D-344R), Dakota System, Vega Sector

**Established:** 2647

**Commander:** Admiral William Wilson

**Executive Officer:** Commodore Lauryn DeLucaz

**Marine Commander:** Colonel Jakob Ybarra

**Space Force Commander:** Commodore Tuesday Frace

**Function:** HQ Vega Fleet Operations

HQ 4th Fleet

HQ 56 Marine Division (CMC)

HQ 32 Space Force (CSF)

**Garrison:** 663rd Fleet Support Group

356th Marine Battalion

232nd Fighter Squadron

**Security Status:** Yellow. No civilian traffic, no families or dependents of military forces.

**Permanent Party Personnel:** 7,000 CN; 4,000 CMC; 2,700 CSF; 800 Civilian Support

**Maximum Capacity:** 25,000

**Spacedock Capacity:** 12 large berths (carrier/tanker), 40 regular berths

**History:** Commissioned by the Confederation Senate Security Committee to act as the primary strategic installation in Vega sector in 2638. Completed in 2646 by the Naval Corps of Engineers. Dedicated as Vega fleet headquarters 2648.037.

Pegasus Naval base has been directly attacked twice by Kilrathi forces, first on 2648.247 and again on 2652.097. Both times the attackers were repulsed by ships of the 4th Fleet with minimal Confed losses.

**Description:** Pegasus is an asteroid base located in the Dakota system, near the Dakota 3 mining colony. It's a multi-level structure hollowed out of the nickel-iron asteroid D-344R, with a total pressurized area of over 7 million cubic meters.

As Vega fleet headquarters, Pegasus offers full drydock facilities and a 1000-bed hospital, plus extensive supply and ammunition depot facilities. It also serves as the primary military communications hub of Vega sector.

Because of its proximity to the front, and its strategic importance, Pegasus is a closed facility, off-limits to all nonessential civilian personnel, including families and dependents. Therefore, all personnel (except senior commanders) are limited by command directive to no more than two standard years continuous service on Pegasus. Naval personnel are rotated between two years on Pegasus and two years at either Icarus Base, in Pephedro system, or Titan Base, Sol system. Other services are rotated as directed by their respective commands.

Because of its high security, Pegasus is the primary Confed installation for testing new assets under battle conditions. Experimental weapons, ships and defensive technologies are regularly deployed from Pegasus for their first forays against the enemy.

Because it exists under micro-gravity conditions, Pegasus is not limited by the armament restrictions which gravity places on planetary installations. The base is protected by more than 200 hardpoint turrets, each incorporating an antimatter gun and a point-defense missile placement. In addition, there are more than 300 standard missile ports around the base. Direct fighter launch is possible from any of four fighter decks. Perimeter defense is provided by a strike force of at least four destroyers stationed within 10-minutes response time at all times. Natural rock provides armor to a depth of 25 to 75 meters over most of the base.

**M14TCN5 Portable Data Reader Unit**

## Admiral Geoffrey Tolwyn: Personal & Confidential

PERSONAL FILES. Not to be opened except with the express written permission of Admiral Tolwyn, or in accordance with the procedures of Sect. D-147 paragraph G of the Security Act of 2649.

# Command Officer Profiles

## *Admiral William Wilson*

*Friends call him: Bill*

**MARITAL STATUS:**
Wife, Arete (dec., 51.11)

**CHILDREN/DEPENDENTS:**
None

**BORN:**
2498.134

**COMMISSIONED:**
22.07 (Academy)

**LAST PROMOTED:**
49.03

**CURRENT ASSIGNMENT:**
Commander, Pegasus Station

**NOTES:**
Golfer (bad), back-slapper, pipe smoker (Sirian Red)

Bill Wilson is an officer of uncommon intelligence and efficiency. As a battleship commander in the Pilgrim conflict he displayed remarkable imagination and courage. His courage remains, but he seems to have lost the spark of inspiration in recent years. Right now, Wilson seems best suited to the role of base commander. I don't think he'd be happy on staff (though he'd make a superior logistics and supply officer), and I don't think he has the fire for fleet command. If he asks for retirement at 35 I'll grant it, if he decides to stay on until he gets his 40 that's all right as well. However, I don't see him getting any further promotions. I could easily see him staying in charge at Pegasus for the duration and beyond.

Not particularly popular with his men, but he keeps discipline. Don't put him too near the action, or too far in the rear—he's exactly the kind of man we need reinforcing the front. Very blunt—keep the press away, and don't let him loose on the Senate without a leash.

There are persistent rumors of a drinking problem. I've looked into them, and they're nonsense, although I suspect he did go through a brief bad time after the death of his wife (note: don't mention Mrs. Wilson unless he does so first—puts him in a bad mood).

I've only had a few private conversations with Wilson, but I suspect he's religious, in a mystical kind of way. Seems to prefer to keep the details to himself.

If he's needed at HQ or on Terra, try to work some golfing time in, does wonders for his morale. I've never seen him happier than after 18 holes with two senators and a general, all equally pathetic at the game.

Also fishes a bit, though he definitely prefers the links. Other than that, doesn't seem to have any hobbies.

# Commodore Richard Bellegarde

*Friends call him: Richard*

**MARITAL STATUS:**
Single

**CHILDREN/DEPENDENTS:**
No dependents

**BORN:**
05.265

**COMMISSIONED:**
29.02 (OCS)

**LAST PROMOTED:**
52.10

**CURRENT ASSIGNMENT:**
Naval Ops Adjunct, HQ Command (Concordia)

**NOTES:**
Beer aficionado, card player, uncomfortable around children, allergic to cats

My Good Right Hand and protégé. Good strategist, and getting better. An excellent man with the press, also knows how to talk to the line captains. Still needs to be reined back a bit around senators and other civilian brass.

Richard came in at the very tag-end of the Pilgrim affair, and some of the other senior officers (particularly those whom he has jumped in rank) like to remind him of this. I believe it's a sore spot. Also doesn't help that he's not an Academy man.

I don't believe I could have tolerated our present strategic waiting-game if it wasn't for Richard's poker-player nerves. He has a samurai's appreciation for offensive inaction. Sometimes, during strategy sessions he gets this far-away look in his eyes and his voice drops almost as though he's talking to himself, and I absolutely know that the next thing he says is going to be devastatingly brilliant. If he ever gets to the place where he can do that regularly and on command, I swear I'll retire the next day and leave the whole bloody war to him.

I have certain doubts about Richard. Not his loyalty per se, nor his commitment to the war effort. Rather, I'm concerned that he does not sufficiently appreciate the importance of Confed—and of Terra itself—as a concept. He sees the present war merely as an Us-vs.-Them survival struggle, without regard to its long-term ramifications to our race and culture. He sees that we must win, but he does not see the ramifications of victory (if we lose, of course, any discussion of the "long term" is strictly a moot point).

Fancies himself a lady's man. Richard has only narrowly avoided scandal more than once. His ongoing career depends on him having put such youthful indiscretions behind him.

Plays cutthroat poker. Shouldn't be allowed to play cards with anybody important who hates to lose.

I'd like to boost Richard a rank and give him a fleet, or perhaps a whole sector, but not until I find somebody who can replace him at his current post. He needs to move up if he's to be ready to take over for me when I retire.

**M14TCN5 Portable Data Reader Unit**

# Commander Paul Gerald

*Friends call him: Paul*

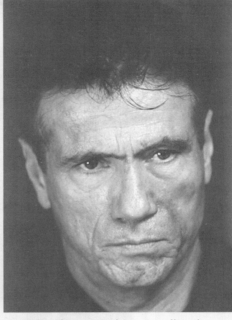

**MARITAL STATUS:**
Divorced (estranged)

**CHILDREN/DEPENDENTS:**
One daughter, Sandy, b. 41.042

**BORN:**
16.198

**COMMISSIONED:**
33.06 (Academy)

**LAST PROMOTED:**
45.01

**CURRENT ASSIGNMENT:**
First Officer, CS Tiger Claw

**NOTES:**
Don't know him well at all. Reported to like camping (Terran & exotic). Competitive marksman in his Academy days.

I've only met Gerald a couple of times. Most of my information is second-hand.

An excellent hard-line, by-the-book XO. I must confess I've dawdled in giving him his own command. According to reports, his crews respect him, but they don't really follow him. Gerald's best when he's paired with a captain who's a good motivator. His day will come soon enough, however. We're simply too short on command-grade officers to not use a man of Gerald's experience.

Reported to be inflexible and a bit prejudiced. Like far too many of our officers who came aboard since the last war, Gerald is all too eager to blame the Pilgrims for everything from crop blight on Brack to the latest advance in Kilrathi fighter tech.

Needs to think more about the war he's in now and less about the one he missed.

Has spent almost all of his career to date aboard carriers in one capacity or another, and by all accounts he knows a flight deck as well as any tech chief in the fleet. I'd like for his first command to be something smaller than a carrier, but I'd fear wasting his strongest expertise. Perhaps a carrier support ship? Staff is another possibility—seems to have a mind for strategy, but I have no evidence the man possesses even a shred of political sensibility.

Biggest asset seems to be an affinity for the care and feeding of pilots. Definitely knows when to slack the leash and when to crack the whip with a fighter wing. The Tiger Claw's wing saw a 23% jump in its efficiency rating in his first year as XO, and continues to climb. His pilots tend to get their jobs done, and also to come back alive, at a significantly better-than-average rate.

# *Captain Lawrence Sansky*

*Friends call him: Ski (dislikes his given name)*

**MARITAL STATUS:**
Single

**CHILDREN/DEPENDENTS:**
No dependents

**BORN:**
04.133

**COMMISSIONED:**
25.03

**LAST PROMOTED:**
40.08

**CURRENT ASSIGNMENT:**
Captain, CS Tiger Claw

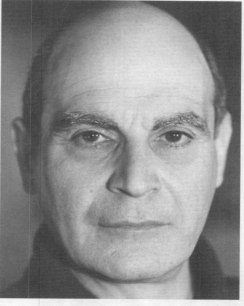

Sansky's crews all seem to adore him. Gossip holds him a soft commander, but I regard that as simple jealousy. His efficiency reports are first rate. He and Gerald make an ideal command team, I think— the father figure and the headmaster.

Sansky seems to be particularly good in a crisis. Several times I've seen him bring his ship back from situations I'd have thought hopeless (he earned himself a Senatorial Star during the Epsilon initiative, while commanding the Halsey), and I consider that final and sufficient indicator of his qualifications as a commander.

As far as I can tell he has no interest whatsoever in further promotion. However, if the need were truly urgent I wouldn't hesitate to give him a fleet (though I'm sure he'd hate it). Likewise, if he ever makes noises about retiring I'd be perfectly happy to boost him to Commodore just to give him the benefits. Seems the least we could do.

**NOTES:**
Excellent darts player, horrid amateur painter, likes musical theater. Very good with brass and press.

I must confess a wholly subjective liking for Sansky. Give him a wooden deck and a new uniform and he'd be right at home in a Hornblower novel. A lifelong bachelor, I really believe he regards himself as married to his ship. If I ever need a replacement for Dwight, I wouldn't mind seeing Sansky at the helm of the Concordia.

In my more sober moments, however, I have to admit that I don't really know Sansky at all, nor have I ever met anyone who claims they do. He's a pleasant fellow to be around, but he's very good at keeping his real self to himself. I respect that in an officer, but it also worries me in a subordinate.

**M14TCN5 Portable Data Reader Unit**

# CN Threat Report K459-C
# Kilrathi Skipper Missile

**Distribute to: All Command Personnel**

**First Issued 2646.252**

**Current Update 2654.071**

## THREAT

Based on intelligence analysis, development by the enemy of the Ultra-Long-Range Phased Photon-Cloak Torpedo, aka "Skipper Missile," has been upgraded from "potential" to "imminent" threat status. This threat may be reasonably expected to appear in the enemy's arsenal within six months to three years.

## DESCRIPTION

The Ultra-Long-Range Phased Photon-Cloak Torpedo (hereafter referred to as the Skipper Missile) is a strategic ship or satellite weapon used for single-strike assaults on installations and cap ships. It may carry high-explosive, nuclear, radiation, antiradiation or exotic warheads.

The Skipper Missile employs a photon cloak to evade counter-measures. The photon cloak uses a linked array of at least three antigraviton emitters to route photons and other electromagnetic emissions around the object with no reflection or diffusion. In effect, the cloaked missile becomes invisible to all electromagnetic sensors, including the human eye.

## WEAKNESSES

As a long-range stealth weapon, the Skipper Missile will probably move quite slowly by ballistic standards—probably more slowly than a starfighter at full acceleration. This means that effective interception may be possible.

As currently envisioned, cloaking technology inhibits sensor operation from both directions. That is, just as it is impossible to see what's in a cloak, it is likewise difficult to see out from within the cloak. Furthermore, early cloak generators may require an exceptional energy output to maintain, particularly in a torpedo-sized object. There is further a likelihood that a working photon cloak will lead to heat and radiation buildup within, since the energy output of the cloaked object cannot dissipate normally. Energy emissions from within a cloaked area will be "caught" in the cloak field and circulate in an increasing feedback loop, eventually leading to shield overload and possibly the destruction of the cloaked object. Early versions of the Skipper Missile, therefore, can be expected to uncloak periodically.

This will allow them to correct their course (particularly against cap ships and other moving objects), and also to vent energy emissions. Because of this "energy vent" effect, Skipper Missiles should appear as "bright spots" on most sensor readouts—they will stand out much more keenly to sensor arrays than other torpedoes and probably most fighter-sized objects. It can be expected, however, that these decloaked periods will be transitory in nature, probably somewhere between 1 and 10 seconds. It can be expected that Skipper Missiles targeted on moving targets (e.g., cap ships) will uncloak for periods somewhat longer than those targeted on stationary or orbital targets (e.g., satellites and installations), due to the necessity of both venting energy and correcting trajectory.

**DEFENSE**

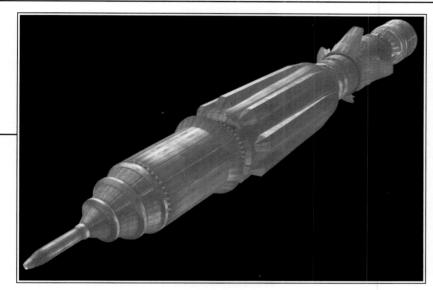

Decloaked Skipper Missiles will be easily detected from most cap ships, at distances up to several hundred thousand kilometers. It is essential, however, that they be recognized for what they are. An intense reading as from a large, slow-moving object that appears suddenly and vanishes after a few seconds may be dismissed as an equipment glitch or transitory astronomical phenomenon.

Operators should be made aware of the possibility that such a reading may represent a Skipper Missile. When such a reading is detected, any fighter escorts should be informed immediately of an unconfirmed bogie, and that sector of space should be monitored carefully for at least 15 minutes for any repeat of the same reading. If a repeat occurs along a rough line between the first reading and any potential target, it should be regarded as a confirmed reading, and full defensive posture adopted.

The most effective defense against skipper technology will probably be fighter interdiction. Fighters have the requisite speed and mobility to close with and destroy a Skipper Missile in the seconds it may be decloaked. Upon notification that a bogie is a possible Skipper Missile, fighters should move to interpose themselves between the target ship and the Skipper, and wait for any more readings while scanning visually for the missile's next decloak. Fast, long-range, low-damage weapons like lasers should prove effective, as it is unlikely an unmanned, torpedo-sized object will mount both cloak and shield technology.

Depending on its warhead, there is a possibility that the destruction of a Skipper Missile may result in spontaneous detonation, possibly causing collateral damage.

Cf. Threat Report K422-B, Kilrathi Stealth Fighter, Updated 2654.012

**M14TCN5 Portable Data Reader Unit**

## Inquiry Into the Loss of the Odysseus-Class Naval Exploratory Vessel CS *Iason* Reg E-1456

### COMPILED FROM STAFF REPORTS, INSPECTOR GENERAL'S OFFICE, CONFEDERATION NAVY 2639.152

**DATE OF LOSS:**

2638.229

**COMMANDER:**

Commander Jedora Andropolos

**RULING AS TO CAUSE:**

Destroyed under fire from hostile ships

**PROBABILITY OF ACCURACY:**

100%

**DEGREE OF LOSS:**

All hands, all cargo and ordnance

**RECOVERABLE SALVAGE:**

None

**FLIGHT RECORDER:**

Not recovered

**SUMMARY:** At 0450 hours on 2638.229, *Iason* made visual contact with three Kilrathi B'ru'k-class merchantmen. For approximately five hours the *Iason* attempted to establish communication with the alien vessels, with no response. During this time the *Iason* maintained a continuous data-stream transmission to CN HQ. About 1000 hours Kilrathi ships opened fire without warning, destroying the *Iason*'s offensive, defensive, drive and life-support capabilities.

**RECOVERY:** At approximately 1900 hours on 2638.234, Kilrathi B'ru'k-class merchantman jumped into Hyperion system towing the gutted hull of the *Iason*. The hull was cut adrift near Hyperion 4, apparently as a challenge or warning. After extensive long- and medium-range scanning, hull was destroyed by friendly fire, by order of Port Admiral Miru, due to the possibility of enemy booby traps.

**SHIP SPECIFICATIONS:** CS *Iason*, commissioned 2613.078 as long-range exploratory vessel, refitted 2633 as fleet support transport, refitted 2637 as exploratory/ research vessel.

Modified Odysseus-class explorer massing 17,000 tons. Jump drive, hopper drive, long-range fusion impulse drive. Enhanced sensor array, ultra-long-range communications system (voice and data), self-sustaining life-support systems rated for 1.2 year voyage @ full complement, astronomy, xenology, planetology and gravitics laboratory facilities.

Armed with 2 twin long-range pulse cannon, one torpedo tube, 12 N44 torpedoes with conventional explosive warheads. Class 5 heavy-carbon armor, 4.7 terajoule xenon-charged phase shield generator.

1 long-range Pelican-class shuttle refitted for research, 1 standard Tern-class shuttle, 2 towed Ferret-class scout fighters with enhanced sensor arrays, 19 lifeboats.

Crew consisting of 19 officers and 71 crew, plus research staff consisting of 3 officers, 19 crew, 5 civilians.

Cargo capacity of 8000 cubic meters, cargo of provisions, research equipment, unknown quantity of research samples.

**DETAIL:** Departed Port of Hellespont 2638.009 on nine-month mapping/ research mission into outer Vega sector. Put in at Tartarus .065 for minor repairs. In continuous communication with HQ for entire voyage.

On .221 *Iason* hopped into system V343 to investigate composition of gas giants in the outer system. When early scans produced evidence of complex radioactives in outer atmosphere of planet 9 (in 11-planet system), Captain Andropolos ordered a 10-day layover for analysis, after which *Iason* was to hop back to Tyr jump point.

At 0450 hours on .229, automatic scanners recorded three unknown objects moving at a high rate of speed on a non-orbital trajectory, at a range of 97,000 kilometers. At 0512 hours objects altered course to intercept vector with *Iason*. By this point scans had already confirmed that the objects were pressurized, manufactured, self-propelled craft of unknown origin. Upon being notified of the approaching ships, Captain Andropolos ordered full shields and readiness standby level 2.

At 0527 unknown craft entered visual range, and the captain ordered continuous wide-band scanning combined with a continuous real-time telemetry stream to HQ. Based on scans and images, craft have since been identified as Kilrathi B'ru'k-class light freighters, armed with heavy mass drivers and anti-ship missiles.

At 0610 captain transmitted formal notice to HQ and Confed of first contact with sentient, non-human spacefarers. This transmission also advised that the *Iason* was monitoring alien radio traffic in unknown language, and had begun hailing procedures according to Confed first contact protocols.

(Recordings of the Kilrathi traffic during this period are fragmentary, and translation is still underway, but it appears to be a discussion of the *Iason*'s nature and offensive capability.)

At 0715 hours both Ferrets were scrambled. One, piloted by Captain F. Izmuti, was ordered to begin a pattern of concentric fly-bys of the Kilrathi ships, while the other, piloted by Commander J. Taggart, was ordered to commence long- and medium-range scans of the area.

At 0743 hours, on an approach within 2 kilometers of the Kilrathi ships, one of the Kilrathi opened fire on Capt. Izmuti's Ferret, damaging the right wing array, including cameras and stabilizers. She was ordered to return to the *Iason*. Commander Taggart remained in space apparently until after the *Iason* was destroyed. His precise fate is unknown.

At 0800 hours Captain Andropolos sent a second message to HQ, indicating she was going to "wait out" the situation, taking no further overt action other than continuing automatic hails on all frequencies, until the Kilrathi took action.

For most of the next hour, the Kilrathi remained silent, even maintaining radio silence between themselves. At 0857 a video signal was transmitted to the *Iason*. Captain Andropolos immediately ordered a two-way channel, but the Kilrathi signal showed only an unadorned wall. It was noted that the signal was largely within the infrared spectrum. It is likely that the Kilrathi wished to get a look at the humans without showing themselves. If that was their intent, it was successful.

At 0942 hours, a Kilrathi radio transmission was intercepted. This has been translated as the order to open fire on the *Iason*. However, its meaning would have been unknown to the ship's crew. The three Kilrathi ships all opened fire simultaneously a few seconds thereafter. Captain Andropolos gave the order to return fire and retreat at top speed. The Kilrathi pursued, keeping pace with the *Iason*.

The signal from the *Iason* continued until 0947, when it broke up, probably due to electromagnetic interference from the battle. Tactical analysis suggests that the *Iason*'s shields would have endured until about 1000 or shortly thereafter. When the shields fell, hull integrity would have been fatally breached within 15 seconds. Most of the crew probably would have died either of radiation flash when the drives exploded, or of oxygen deprivation due to depressurization. If any of the crew made it to the lifeboats or into full-environment suits, they were probably killed by subsequent Kilrathi boarding parties. The possibility of living captives being taken cannot be ruled out, although this does not appear to be normal procedure after Kilrathi victories.

At 0130 hours sector HQ certified the *Iason* as a lost or missing ship.

On 2638.234 at about 1900 hours, a single B'ru'k-class ship jumped through the Hyperion jump point towing an object slightly larger than itself by volume. It proceeded at full speed into the system up to the orbit of the fourth planet, disconnected from its cargo at 2307, and returned at full speed to the jump point, leaving the system at about 0200 hours on .235. The Kilrathi ship was identified only by long-range scanners at the jump point, and was never within visual range of any Confed ship or monitor. It is not known if it was one of the three which attacked the *Iason*.

Ships were dispatched from Hyperion 2 to investigate the object, and at 0512 hours on .236 it was formally identified as the *Iason*. Port Admiral Miru, of Hellespont Naval Station, reached the scene in the CS *Kurosawa* at 1500 hours. Over the next 16 hours the hull was extensively scanned by Navy sensor teams, but Admiral Miru ordered a quarantine distance of 10 kilometers. No Confed personnel were allowed within that distance.

Scans revealed that there were no living or dead humans on the hulk, and furthermore that the Kilrathi had stripped the ship virtually down to bare hull walls. At 0700 hours on .237, the admiral ordered scanning stopped. Based on the risk of biological or other contamination of the hulk by the Kilrathi, the admiral ordered the hulk to be tractored to a descending spiral orbit into Hyperion's star, and further ordered that once such orbit was achieved, the hulk should be destroyed by torpedo fire. Based on ballistic projections, the debris from the *Iason* fell into the star and were destroyed on or about 2638.244.

CONCLUSION: *Iason* lost due to attack by superior hostile force. The actions of the captain and crew are deemed by this office to have been in accordance with the policies and traditions of the Confederation Navy, and this report is referred to Command for consideration for posthumous honors.

IP Port Status: un**docked**    OP Port Status: un**docked**

Clearance Key Status: insertcard_verifying_denied_**accepted**

Data Security Level: unclassified_confidential_secret_**topsecret**

 View  Store  Delete

## PSYCHOLOGICAL PROFILE

As per your request, I have interviewed Lt. Christopher Blair, with a view towards . . .

 View  Store  Delete

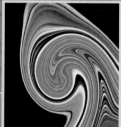

## PILGRIM POWERS

It has come to our attention that a student of Progress University has been researching the appearance of Navigational powers . . .

 View  Store  Delete

## NAVCOM A.I.

Excerpts from *Advanced Theories of Space Navigation*, Confederation Academy Publishing (Terra) . . .

SEARCH  PREV  NEXT  RELOAD  SAVE  PRINT  QUIT

View  Store  Delete

### INQUIRY INTO THE CAPTURE AND SUBSEQUENT ESCAPE AND RETURN OF CMDR. TAGGART

View  Store  Delete

### CORRESPONDENCE: TAGGART TO TOLWYN
How do you like the new letterhead? I'm greatly looking forward to beginning my adventures as a Free Trader . . .

TOP SECRET

query "top_secret update" media=org_top, level=TOP_SECRET | return=5
. . . Retrieving 5 text files + graphical subfiles . . .

Your search is being monitored and recorded. Keying search #153TS . . .
Reference this search code to recall articles.
Please insert data chip . . . You may view, store, or delete.

    article 1 of 5="cn academy security report, christopher blair"
    article 2 of 5="intelligence, pilgrim powers"
    article 3 of 5="navcom"
    article 4 of 5="escape, taggart"
    article 5 of 5="correspondence, taggart to tolwyn"

**M14TCN5 Portable Data Reader Unit**

Please insert security chip......Analyzing......Chip accepted......With valid passcode you can be cleared to......Top Secret level.....Chip access limited by logon ID....Recall logon ID......
ID=23098799m707.....Searching access files....ID matches file.......Security level clearance accepted

## Office of Special Psychological Operations
### *Colonel Jillian Ickes, M.D.*

**TO: ADMIRAL GEOFFREY TOLWYN**

**RE: PSYCHOLOGICAL PROFILE OF CHRISTOPHER BLAIR**

**2653.103**

Sir,

As per your request, I have interviewed Lt. Christopher Blair, with a view towards any potential security risk involving enemy psychological exploitation of trauma related to the death of his parents, or his mother's Pilgrim heritage.

I interviewed the Lt. on three separate occasions (.084, .092, .099 of this year) at the SF Flight School on Sirius, for periods of 60 minutes each. The interviews were conducted under the guise of a research study into the early motivational factors of pilot candidates. I also interviewed three of Blair's classmates at the same time, to substantiate my cover and act as control subjects. I chose to interview the subject just after mid-cycle exams—a time of minimal training stress.

I have no reason to believe that either the Lt. or his school superiors suspected that Blair was the target of any special inquiry.

SCREEN 2 | query "cn academy security report, christopher blair"
source=Office of Special Psychological Operations, 2653.103

## PROFILE: CHRISTOPHER BLAIR

Despite a mild defensive reaction upon first mention of his mother, once he was satisfied that I had no observable prejudice towards Pilgrims in general, Blair proved quite eager to discuss his parents. This is, generally speaking, a positive sign—had he been evasive or sullen on the subject, that would have been a far more ominous indicator.

Lt. Blair definitely has deep-seated feelings of rejection and guilt over the death of his parents. As a small child he harbored the irrational belief that he had somehow caused his parents to "go away," and that he could somehow "bring them back" through correct behavior. Such childhood feelings are quite common in those orphaned at a young age, and they inevitably leave a deep impression on the adult psyche.

Blair was smuggled off Peron as an infant, and sent to live with his father's sister's family. His parents were both killed in the siege of Peron—an event which occurred when Blair was four. His early school years fell during the immediate post-war era, a time when wartime jingoism remained high. He gained a good deal of self-esteem and peer acceptance from the fact that his father was a war hero who had been killed in action. (Blair did not find out until much later that his father was actually killed during an unauthorized attempt to rescue his mother—these details were suppressed in the account of the death released to the family, apparently for compassionate reasons.) He was kept ignorant of his mother's background and, like many post-war children (and indeed, many adults), he learned to demonize Pilgrims as treacherous, savage totalitarians.

Under these circumstances, he could not have discovered the truth about his mother at a worse time, or in a worse way. Shortly before his eighth birthday, his mother's origins were discovered by a reporter, who published a sensational story titled "War Hero's Secret Pilgrim Romance" to the sector news-nets. The story identified the Blairs by name, and prominently mentioned that the union produced a son, who was living on Blair's colony. The community was both rural and conservative, and the revelation created a disproportionate scandal. In a shocking display of irrational prejudice, the parents of several of Blair's close playmates instructed their children to stop associating with him. Of course, he was mocked severely by the same children who had formerly lionized him as a hero's son.

**M14TCN5 Portable Data Reader Unit**

This incident constitutes the second significant trauma of Blair's childhood. It revived his early feelings of guilt and abandonment in a more mature and articulate context (the adult Blair is able to describe memories of his emotions from this time in great detail). If his mother was an "evil" Pilgrim, did that mean that he was evil, too? If his father loved his mother, did that make the father a "traitor"? During this period Blair's grades (which had been excellent) plummeted, and he began to become withdrawn, stubborn, and destructive. (In our interviews, Blair confirmed these reactions, but also expressed the opinion that his school reports from the period were exaggeratedly negative, due to his teachers' prejudice and reduced expectations of excellence.)

From that nadir his grades and conduct showed a steady increase over the next several years. As the community got over its initial shock at Blair's parentage, he was able to resume his emotional development. Nonetheless, his emotional scars continued to retard his progress.

Blair himself identifies his 13th year as the time in which he determined to move beyond his parentage. By this time the Kilrathi had replaced the Pilgrims as the popular demons of choice, and the media was becoming more objective in its assessments of the Pilgrim culture. Some were even beginning to publicly raise serious questions about Confed's own motivations and ethics in the Pilgrim conflict.

In this environment Blair was able to channel his adolescent rebelliousness and natural intelligence into an intense search for the "truth" about his parents. He read voraciously on the Pilgrim Conflict—popular history, Confed propaganda, radical revisionist propaganda and militaria were all pursued avidly. It is at this time that he began to surreptitiously wear the Pilgrim cross inherited from his mother (which had been recovered along with his parents' bodies). His intellectual fascination with the period of his parents' death continues to this day, and appears to be the cornerstone of his personal coping mechanism against his childhood traumas.

In high school his grades again rose. His only reported behavioral problems during this time involve argumentativeness in class, and several variations on the theme of "holding unconventional/unpopular views in a conservative community." This intellectual individualism did not prevent him from becoming a class leader and successful athlete.

He says he did not know whether or not he would apply for Academy appointment until the day of the deadline. According to Blair himself, he did not want to become an officer until he was "certain he was 100% behind it." His Academy record indicates that he did commit himself completely to his goal, once he determined to act upon it.

## CONCLUSIONS

Lt. Blair has unquestionably been traumatized by his early losses and the childhood humiliation associated with the revelation of his Pilgrim heritage. There is likewise no question that a skilled psychological operative could, through a concentrated program of hypnotism, role-playing and physical abuse and deprivation, turn these tendencies into a full-blown psychosis, probably involving intense feelings of hatred towards Confed.

**SCREEN 4 | query "cn academy security report, christopher blair"**
**source=Office of Special Psychological Operations, 2653.103**

As I am sure the admiral is aware, however, it is axiomatic to those in my profession that everybody has such early traumas, which can be manipulated through sufficiently concerted modifications to produce virtually any desired behavior. The meaningful question is not whether Blair possesses exploitable psychological weaknesses (a tautology, from my viewpoint), but whether these vulnerabilities represent any unusual risk.

In my opinion they do not. Were I, for example, assigned to compromise Blair's unit, my initial line of attack would certainly be an attempt to introduce certain members of the unit to attractive members of the opposite sex (nor would Blair be among my first choices in this regard). Furthermore, if I actually did try a complicated and expensive course of radical behavior modification on Lt. Blair, it would be far more likely to leave him a vegetable than to produce a functional psychopathic operative with exploitable neurosis.

I do feel that there is some risk that Blair's traumas may assert themselves under combat stress. He does display a certain militancy towards his mother's background (he wears her Pilgrim cross at all times) and if his Pilgrim connections bring him into suspicion—particularly under the insular conditions of a warship—it may trigger a reversion to his childhood rejection traumas, resulting in an erosion of discipline and moral, and perhaps even violence. Such risks should more properly be assessed within a psychotherapeutical environment.

Moving on to the question of Blair's present loyalties and motivations, I see little cause for alarm there, either.

Blair is an intelligent young man with a complex personal morality. He has deliberately exposed himself to, and rationally evaluated, most of the radical philosophies of the present and recent past. After this research, he chose to become a Confed officer when he was, in his words, "certain he was 100% behind it." His loyalty to Confed is neither unreserved nor unconditional; however, it is conscious, rational and, in my opinion, deeply felt.

Regarding his feeling towards the Pilgrims, he has carefully cultivated a neutral viewpoint towards the Pilgrim conflagration. This is a coping mechanism related to his feelings towards his mother, but it is also a rational and informed viewpoint. Blair does not see the Pilgrim war in terms of good and bad, but as a dispassionate political and philosophical struggle. While he apparently respects the sincerity of the Pilgrim faith, I saw no sign that he had any personal inclination towards Pilgrim dogma (and, in fact, Blair displays some amusement at the more outré manifestations of the Pilgrim faith). He did express some frustration at the dearth of objective reports on the Pilgrim religion and culture (as opposed to the history of the Pilgrim conflict) in the popular media.

To summarize, I find no special security risks in Blair's background or psychological makeup. I do not recommend any further observation or any restriction of his career as a pilot or Confederation officer.

Respectfully submitted,

**M14TCN5 Portable Data Reader Unit**

FROM: COMMANDER YONSON, CIS                    2641.252
TO: ADMIRAL TOLWYN

*Sir,*

*It has come to our attention that a student of Progress University has been researching the appearance of Navigational powers exhibited throughout the history of space exploration. This information is accurate, and is a veritable road map for some of the advanced theories inherent to the NAVCOM A.I.*

*Fortunately, damage control will be possible. She has been contacted, has accepted a position at Akwende, and has agreed to suppress her findings for the foreseeable future. We are in the process of cleaning up the historical records which allowed her to come to these conclusions.*

*I have included a summary of her dissertation below.*

# A Theory on the Origin and History of Extraordinary Navigational Powers

*Researched, compiled, and interpreted by Lang Tanaka, in partial fulfillment of the requirements specified by Progress University, Semester II, 2641.*

## INTRODUCTION

It is my intention to prove to the discriminating mind that the vaunted "Pilgrim Navigational Abilities" are neither the result of a divine gift nor the inexplicable luck of a madman and blindly devoted followers. Rather, I will attempt to explain the phenomenon as the consequence of genetic mutation engendered by non-Terran conception, gestation and birth.

Due to the political and emotional nature of the philosophies, accomplishments and subsequent martial stance of the Pilgrims, I find it necessary to preface this paper with a definition.

> **Mutation (n.)** 1. The sudden change of characteristics which are genetically inherited, and cannot be traced to previous generations. 2. Any difference in the chromosomal makeup of a germ cell that was not previously extant in the parent organism. 3. Any change in form, qualities or characteristics.

Mutation is the inherent mechanism that allows any growing organism to adapt to new environments and conditions. It has proven vital for the survival of Homo sapiens in the various climates and levels of civilization found within the relatively nurturing atmosphere of Terra. It is what has allowed us humans to survive millennia of change, and to thrive in a variety of disparate environments.

While I cannot insist that any reader using this work as reference material do so in the spirit which I intended, I insist that wherever my name, or this report, is referenced, the following footnote must be appended:

*It is the opinion of Lang Tanaka that the mutation of the Pilgrims does not constitute the creation of a new species of being, but merely a new race of man.*

## History of Space Syndrome Mutation

### EARLY TESTS

The earliest studies of the effects of non-Terran conception, gestation and birth that were begun during the late 20th century were largely inconclusive. These mostly consisted of experiments on animals (primarily mice, although one experiment using primates has been reported). Conditions in space were not optimal, and the political pressure on Terra was such that, not only did they feel it necessary to perform the experiments in complete secrecy, but 73.2% of the experiments (both space-based, and Terran-based controls) were considered "tainted" by biased researchers.

## SCREEN 2 | query "intelligence, pilgrim powers" | source=Progress University, Sem II, 2641

However, while the results were inconclusive, the resultant opinion was that low-G and zero-G procreation was feasible. Granting that the data was flawed, it was noted that conception was more likely to fail (an estimated 22% under fertile conditions), birth complications were increased (19%), and there were an array of psychological effects on the gravid animal. These were attributed to the zero-G conditions. Notably, genetic "defects" were considered within the range of average, with any variation from the norm being statistically nonexistent.

When similar tests were performed in 2173, on Phobos Station [Dr. Monzoli, Report 217, 2173.118], the results were very different. Conception and complications fell to within normal range, with no unusual psychological effects on record. The station, it should be noted, had a centrifugal gravity of .6 G. The statistics on record show that the stillbirth rate was 4% higher than the norm, but this was apparently considered cause for neither concern nor autopsy. When later experiments were conducted on Olympia Station using Rhesus monkeys [Drs. Gray and Bauer, Report 682, 2175.336], results were similar. Normal conception and birth ranges, and slightly elevated stillbirth rate, with a sub-note that one of the resultant males showed psychotic tendencies and had to be killed. Subsequent generations showed similar elevations in stillbirths, and a recurring, but not consistent, level of psychosis. [Dr. Gray, Reports 20, 55, 72 and Dr. Bauer, Report 22]

Unmentioned in their reports is that at least two of the monkeys escaped and defied capture for several months, living in the crawlspaces between various bulkheads and decks until starved out. [Station Maintenance Reports 2175.053-152]

Meanwhile, tests were underway to determine what effects local-space travel had on pregnant women. Results were conclusive that even the high-G forces involved in acceleration and deceleration were harmless to a healthy fetus [Space Exploration and Colonization Council, Houston, Press Release 2175.077], and the door was opened to colonization lobbying.

Despite obvious reluctance to go on record as approving human procreation in space, there was enormous public and political pressure to begin colonization of space, and both Drs. Gray and Bauer concluded that there was no real danger for pregnant women, certified by the SECC, to travel off-planet. They did add the caveat that they considered the subject to be under-researched, and lobbied the United Nations to fund further tests. The funding did not materialize, although subsequent notes by station physicians provide a great deal of information for the historical researcher.

### CONDITIONS

By the year 2250, there were nineteen fully functional space stations in Sol system, and while all but two of them (Luna and Phobos) were designed with the possibility of an internally expanding population (i.e., children) in mind, few were able to live up to the reality. The academic zones were rarely used for the purpose they had been intended, almost universally being reclaimed for extra cargo space (Mimas), additional living quarters (Eros), manufacture (Titan and Neptune) or whatever seemed important at the time.

Schooling became more practical than academic, with a system of apprenticeship becoming very common, and the liberal arts and other "traditional" subjects being reserved for those whose parents could afford vids and tutors.

Small children, from infancy until the age of six or seven, spent their time either with their parents at their occupations (the "Timmy Tether"—an elastic leash for tying children to their parents or to "safe" areas—gained popularity on Titan, and was quickly adopted on all other stations), or in "Wild Hall"—a kind of recess area where one or more adults supervised the children at play. After the age of seven, they were assigned to menial jobs in various departments, working their way through increasing levels of task difficulty until they could pass the exams that would enable them to enter the professional workforce. Work hours were strictly regulated, for children as for adults, and rarely exceeded ten hours per 24-hour standard day. Literacy was surprisingly universal, usually learned at home from vid programs. [Rose Sicilliano, Born in Heaven: The Life of a Station Child, Twelfth Press, 2592]

After half a dozen generations had been born in space, the social dynamics began to change considerably. Gradually, castes and ghettos began to form. The less vital, or intellectual, an occupation, the closer to the hull of the ship were the assigned living quarters. Pay ranges varied little between occupational "levels," and so at first there was little besides the location of the home suites to distinguish the various groups. Clothing, jewelry, foodstuffs and other amenities were equally available—and limited—to all station personnel. Over time, however, hairstyles, dialect jargon and, especially, living quarters began to diverge. [Guillermo Sanchez, Caste Societies, D'bell Associates, 2623] With this divergence came the first real evidence of Space Syndrome Mutation.

**M14TCN5 Portable Data Reader Unit**

## EMERGENCE OF MUTATIONS

In space, population load is an ongoing logistical concern. Early space stations especially could not afford to spend resources, either tangibles such as food or intangibles such as time, on non-productive personnel.

All people who received living visas for space stations were gene-typed. Those who applied for parenting permits were again gene-typed and cross-checked for potential problems. Within a few weeks after conception, the embryo was checked for genetic imperfections, and any "unviable" embryos were either aborted or returned *in vivo* to Terra.

This routine was set on Luna station in the earliest stages of space colonization, and was adopted universally as each new station went on-line.

It was actually noted in the early days of colonization *[Dr. Synatschk, Mutations: Occurrences and Causes, Luna Station, 2189]* that the number of mutations was unusual, not just in comparison to Terran statistics, but specifically in light of the fact that all parents were first gene-typed to prevent such an occurrence. The gist of the report was that lower gravity, stress, and a lack of dietary trace minerals combined to create a heightened level of pre-birth defects. Dr. Synatschk's paper was well-researched and eloquent, and was accepted as the authoritative work on the subject for decades. Statistics varied from station to station, and this was attributed to varying levels of stress, gravity, etc.

It wasn't until 2244 that K. J. Ludwick, an administrative assistant in the Human Resources and Recruitment Division, noticed a correlation. The ratio of unviable embryos increased the closer to the station's hull the mother lived. Upon closer examination, ratios also increased the closer to the edge of the solar system the space station was situated, with a decrease for those stations with unusually thick hulls. Radiation was considered, faulty air or food supplies were investigated, employment conditions were studied. *[See Appendix A, section I, for a list of studies.]*

Nonetheless, there was little outcry since there were far more "normal" conceptions than abnormal ones, and procedures were in place to prevent things from getting out of hand. The phenomenon was eventually attributed to the mysterious (and probably non-existent) Planck Radiation, labeled "Unavoidable" and dealt with on a case-by-case basis.

# Indicators of SS Savants, pre-2500

## CHANGES IN THE GENOME

Space Syndrome Mutation would have had a great deal more press, and a predominant place in history, if the mutated embryos had been brought to term. In fact, miscarriages, short lifespans and misshapen humans would have been common occurrences if events had been allowed to take their natural course. Missing or extra limbs, bone deformities, cardio-circulatory predicaments, nearly anything that could go wrong with a developing body might be expected to surface eventually. Instead, there was a simple outbreak of preventative medical procedures and pharmaceuticals. No need to become alarmed, the community was told. Disappointed parents were encouraged to try again, and after 2244, to try taking up a temporary residence inward.

However, only those genetic imperfections being screened for were being caught. *[Eros Station Medical Procedures Manual, 2247, Section 3, pages iv – xxvii]* Physical deformations were under scrutiny. Unusual abilities or characteristics that manifested throughout individuals' lifetimes were not.

Nevertheless, there are some indications that abilities were also beginning to mutate. Nothing especially unheard of, but when added up, an unusually high count of unusual traits and characteristics were being recorded.

When comparing each generation with the previous generation (a generation being a period of 25 years), there are some facts we can point out as irrefutable:

- The tallest people were taller, the shortest people were shorter
- Healing times were on average faster
- Onset of puberty occurred later
- Gestation took longer
- Psychosis (particularly schizophrenic paranoia and Multiple Personality Syndrome) manifested more often

*[Appendix A, Section III]*

These statistics are not quoted to claim that humans were "evolving" to some "new stage" in human development, but to prove that mutations were undoubtedly being introduced into the genome.

## Emergence of Abilities as Mutations

By the mid-23rd century, certain abilities were being recognized in the ever-changing lingo of the stationers. To a large extent, these referred to people previously known as Savants.

The varieties of Savants to be found on the intra-system space stations ranged from the useful to the merely odd. "Zappers" were those able to quickly locate electrical or physical breakdowns in the station's systems. "Chipheads" were able to engineer flawless hardware designs, to the micro-level, faster than the best computer systems. A "Toolkit" seemed preternaturally able to fix things with whatever unlikely supplies were at hand. "Crunchers" could handle complex mathematical calculations without the use of computers. "Rabbitfoots" were said to bring luck to missions (although there is no empirical evidence to support this last). By the end of the 23rd century, these abilities were common enough that it was possible for the Recruitment divisions to hire for specific abilities.

Also from that period of time, there is evidence that one of the abilities considered interesting but not particularly useful was the "Compass." People with this ability had an astonishing sense of direction, being able to tell instantly where nearby astronomical objects were located. On a station where "down" is merely the direction that the station's gravity is pulling, a Compass could always point directly toward the center of the nearest planet or star. [Mimas Human Resources Precedent & Protocol Manual: Job Descriptions, version 8, 2280]

## Indicators of Advanced SS in Pilgrims, post-McDaniel

Ivar Chu McDaniel's following of believers began to form at the very onset of the 24th century. Although originally small in number, it eventually grew into an active cult following known as the Pilgrim movement.

While it is unknown whether he specifically recruited Savants to join him in his exploratory quest, it is known that he first began to preach his vision at Neptune station, which was the farthest station from Sol and had perhaps the highest concentration of Savants per capita. People from all walks of life joined him, and we have to assume that, with the new emphasis on exploration and the high percentage of Savants on Neptune station, at least a few of his followers would have the Compass ability.

That the Pilgrims had an unusually high survival rate during the infant years of the Morvan Drive is historical fact. [Neptune Station logs 2310-2344] Early Confed sloship missions had a success rate of only 91%, while followers of McDaniel enjoyed closer to 99% success.

On Terra, Savants were only just beginning to be seen as having extra-normal abilities. Prior to 2300, Savants were simply considered "skilled" or "geniuses." They were considered to be experts in their fields, certainly, but nothing more. It wasn't until the McDanielists, as they were then known, began to openly refer to Savants—and particularly the Compasses—as "the Graced," that the Savants were seen as a phenomenon worthy of research.

Projects were funded, research was begun . . . and rumors were spread. There is no known evidence that any procedures more radical than chem-scans and brain-wave analysis were performed. In fact, hard evidence to the contrary exists. [Census of the Outer Planets 2304-2328] (There is good reason to believe that rumors of gene-screening originated with the Pilgrim movement, which was openly interested in recruiting Savants.) Regardless of the source of the rumors, Savants emigrated or went underground. Perhaps if the research had continued as planned, more conclusive results would have resulted. As it was, no abnormalities were reported. Nevertheless, the full emigration had begun. The Pilgrim Alliance was established on Beacon in 2325. By 2360 they had a fleet larger than any commercial firm, with nearly half as many ships as Terran Federal.

The point of interest here is that Pilgrims encouraged Savants to intermarry and procreate, and by the end of the century had reason to sub-categorize Compasses. There were three types of Compass abilities: the Visionary, the Explorer and the Navigator. According to information available from the Pilgrim libraries, the Visionary's ability was in determining which systems would prove most valuable to expansion, while the Explorer's ability was to navigate a sloship safely through unknown and possibly treacherous environments. Explorers also were responsible for the holo-cartography of new territories. Navigators seemed to be able to expertly navigate any territory which had already been explored, notably without the use of traditional computational or cartographic aid. If an Explorer had passed through an area safely, so could a Navigator.

It was partially due to this variety of phenomenon that the Pilgrims gradually came to believe that they were "graced" by the universe, with a manifest destiny of exploration and colonization.

**M14TCN5 Portable Data Reader Unit**

## Summary of Parallel Tonality

The scientists of Terra were not inclined to believe this "divine" version of the Pilgrims' abilities. Research projects were funded, staffed and maintained over a period of more than 200 years. A variety of reports have recently been made public, and while most are undoubtedly still under the deepest degrees of classification, there is still quite a lot to be gleaned.

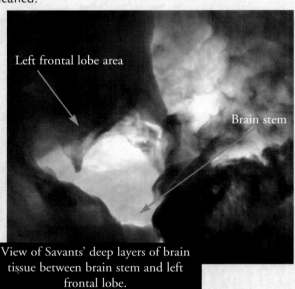

Left frontal lobe area

Brain stem

View of Savants' deep layers of brain tissue between brain stem and left frontal lobe.

The first notable discovery is that the brains of most Savants, particularly those born in the farthest reaches of space, have an unusual pattern of convolutions in the brain. Unlike most human brains, where the pattern of convolutions is fairly evenly distributed, there is a "patchiness" in Savants. Savants have deeper and more intricately folded layers of tissue, notably near the brain stem and the left frontal lobe. These do not seem to respond to external or internal stimuli any more than on a non-Savant human, or even seem particularly necessary to the functions of the subject. Decades went by without any advancement of the theory of how the Compasses "worked."

The breakthrough came when Dr. Kyu Park discovered a series of experiments that had taken place in the year 2153. "Parallel Tonality" had once been of passing interest in the pseudo-science circles, being posited as an explanation of telepathy and the popular theories of reincarnation. *[Parallel Tonality: Ramifications Regarding the Exploratory Endeavor, Dr. Park, Yosu University Press, 2489]*

Although the original experiments had been ridiculed, Dr. Park was intrigued by the idea, and applied it to the conundrum of the Pilgrims' extraordinary abilities. More advanced scientific techniques were available, and it proved to be key in unlocking half of the Pilgrim mysteries: how Navigators were able to "know" what previous Explorers had encountered.

The human brain, it was suggested, was not a device for storing information, but rather was a tool which scripted information onto a parallel dimension, dubbed the "Tanque Dimension," similar to the way an info-vid burner downloaded its data onto a data-chip. It was conceptualized as a series of vibrations, like a musical tone, that were etched into a parallel dimension, and instantly frozen—hence the name Parallel Tonality. Afterwards the same brain would then be able to "read" the information it had scripted. This explained the phenomenon of memories "lost" with the removal of brain tissue being recovered over time; as the brain rewired itself, it relearned its ability to read what it had previously written.

## Summary of "Dead" Dimensions

The concept of parallel dimensions was certainly not new to the 27th century. It had long been understood that while humans could perceive only four dimensions—the material world's three dimensions and time—there could easily be more, beyond human conception and experience. In fact, there have been a small number of scientists throughout history who made a study of the "dead" dimensions, a purely academic study with little practical application, or so it was universally thought.

Dead dimensions were physical dimensions that were created simultaneously with the still-extant four, at the very beginning of the universe . . . but that did not survive the outward expansion of the super-heated universe. The ongoing hypothesis was that as many as two dozen extra dimensions had been born with the universe, but were ripped away to wither and warp into nearly infinitely-small dimensions, to lie hidden somewhere in the dusty corners of the universe. There was a small but devoted scientific following which diligently searched the universe for signs of where these tiny dead dimensions could be found. Theoretically, they alone could answer the question "What happened in the minute which preceded the creation of everything?"

In the 27th century, scientists believe they may have found, if not the locations of the dead dimensions, at least a road sign to the general neighborhood. Despite mankind's reach for the stars and subsequent exploration and colonization, most of the extraordinary astronomical events were still far from mankind's grasp . . . so far away in fact, that astronomers and theoretical physicists were limited to observing events that had happened millions of years ago. Sloships were fast, and went far, but not very far or fast on a universal scale. Space was still a tether, keeping scientists peering out at the universe through a lens that only looked out by looking back in time.

The Akwende Drive changed that. Suddenly, scientists had access to information about a universe that existed, that was essentially close enough to watch, and nearly close enough to touch. Research stations were built next door to the galaxy's Great Mysteries, and overnight, theoretical physics was far from theoretical.

For the Space Exploration program, undoubtedly the most important unexpected discovery was not only proof that the dead dimensions existed, and indeed existed everywhere simultaneously, but that they could actually be stretched into existence by the myriad and grand-scale stresses that were created by the galaxy's largest event-locations: super-novae, black holes, pulsars, wormholes, and the like.

The first discovery was made by an expatriate Pilgrim Alliance scientist, who had voluntarily defected to Terra, asking for and receiving amnesty and a position of research at Mars University.

In light of this new discovery, further research revealed that different galactic events stretched different "dead" dimensions in different ways, and that these differences were perceivable to Explorer Pilgrims.

Just how was difficult to explain, but it was compared to people who, after undergoing relatively simple eye surgery, were somehow able to see in the ultra-violet range of light.

They couldn't describe the experience in normal terms ("bluer than blue, brighter than black"), or see well enough to walk across an area strewn with obstacles, but the actual perception was nonetheless there. The Pilgrims could "see" distortions in space by the varying layers of dead dimensions stretched across them. Over time, and after a great deal of financial resources had been thrown at the project, so could Terran navigational computers.

## Conclusion

Physiological and historical fact, when stripped away from jingoistic political stances, does not allow for the spontaneous creation of a new species. Religious fervor may sway people into believing that they have "ascended" into a new being; wartime suspicions and patriotism may convince people that the opposing side is made up of monsters and something "other" than themselves.

There is ample documentation that Pilgrims were born of mankind, during a time when exposures to unknown dangers were high and genetic mutations commonplace, and death swift to those who mutated in disadvantageous directions. It is, and has always been, a survival trait of the human species to adapt by mutation, to grow to fit our environment, or to die in the attempt.

Just as endomorphic and ectomorphic traits are evolutionary branches in the human species, created by the pressures of environment and the inability for the unfit to survive long enough to procreate, so are the documented changes exhibited by the Pilgrims. These identical pressures come to bear on those who emigrated to space many centuries ago.

The Pilgrims are a new race of man, but just as height or melanin levels may have at one time answered an environmental need, without denying the carriers of their humanity, so too are the Pilgrims to be accepted into varied and complex ranks of Homo sapiens, no better and no worse than the rest of us.

Please insert security chip......Analyzing......Chip accepted......Classified...available only to registered
Confed Navigational Officer courses......logon ID....Recall logon ID=23098799m707...... Searching
access files....ID matches file.......Secure channel transmission only.........Clearance accepted.........

# NAVCOM A.I.

[Excerpted from *Advanced Theories of Space Navigation,* Confederation Academy Publishing (Terra), 5th Edition, San Francisco, 2651.]

As the Akwende Propulsion system was the path to the human race's freedom, the powerful NAVCOM system is the torch that lights the way.

Prior to the discovery of jump drives in 2588, the human race had been locked within the borders of its own solar system. Hostile Pilgrim forces had taken Terra hostage by use of armed sloships, demanding and receiving all rights to the nearest 300 light-years. They enforced with violence any breach of treaty, regardless of intent. Notable episodes included the *Iskander*, a diplomatic envoy which attempted to make independent contact with the Pilgrim Alliance, as well as the two damaged ships *Roxanne* and *Twelfth Rose*, which were ruthlessly destroyed by Pilgrim patrols. They had demanded space for themselves, and would accept no breach of the contract.

Humans, with little choice in the matter, resigned themselves to either dome colonization or micro- and macro-scale terraforming of Sol system's hostile worlds.

The bold destiny of the human race to expand and explore had been limited to half a dozen unsuitable planets, and twice that number of inflexible and fragile station colonies. If it were not for the native ingenuity of the humans, such a small place would still be our domain, left only to peer through space at the rest of the galaxy beyond.

## THE JUMP DRIVE

The Akwende Propulsion system, otherwise known as the "jump drive," was developed by the Aerospatiale Afrique Research Laboratory in 2588. Aerospatiale Afrique Laboratories, situated in the Lower African Republic, has been known throughout the Sol System as the premier location for theoretical scientists since its conception in the year 2201. Never truly intended for direct practical application, the Astronomy division was devoted to pure scientific research until the possible results of their work was made clear to the Terran government.

"Effects and Ramifications of Anti-Graviton Dispersal, Conducted in a Suppressed-Gravity Environment" was the title of Akwende's original report, written in 2214, which started science down the long path that would eventually lead to the discovery of the millennium. It was the first in a long series of papers that served to document the activity of this highly theoretical, yet intensely useful, ivory tower.

## PARALLEL TONALITY

The most recent technology available to navigational computation is Parallel Tonality. This area of science is not a recent discovery, although the practical application of this previously theoretical science is unprecedented.

Theories on Parallel Tonality have existed for centuries. Evidence, in the form of unexplained phenomenon, has existed for millennia. For nearly as long as humankind has existed, the concept of reincarnation has been a prevalent religious concept—the belief that a human lives one life, dies, and then is "reborn" into a new body and a new life. There have been countless cases of people remembering details from past lives, a few verifiable, most not.

Similarly, telepathy—the ability to read another person's thoughts—is a long-established concept. Apparitions, or "ghosts," are also phenomena in the same vein. All have to do with one human somehow sensing what another human has done, with the ordinary five senses somehow bypassed.

At certain points in every century, some form of investigation has been attempted to explain this conundrum. The answer has only recently been made clear: Parallel Tonality.

Through long and painstaking research, it is now clear that the human brain is not, precisely, the organ it was originally—and primitively—assumed to be. It is a neurological computation device, the organ with which all humans "think." Along with a variety of glands, the brain maintains the daily functions of the body. Emotions and complex reactions originate in this intricate array of tissue and nerves. It is a temporary "way station" for short-term memories. This much has nearly always been assumed, and is true.

It is not, however, where memories are stored. Instead, it is a subtle and marvelous device for recording memories onto an associated field, likened to recording vibrations onto a magnetic surface. This field is similar to but different from a gravitational or magnetic field, inasmuch as it is unique to the object that creates it. Unlike other fields currently understood, when the object which created it (the body/brain of the specific human) is removed, the field remains. In this sense, it acts more like an independently extant field, which is utilized, but not created, by the human brain.

The organ can then, at will, read back the stored information. This accounts for how memories which were lost when part of the cerebellum was removed can

**M14TCN5 Portable Data Reader Unit**

eventually be remembered. Once the brain regains the ability to read previously stored information, the information is again available. It was never actually stored in the tissue of the body itself.

Under normal circumstances, an individual brain can only access the information which it itself has "scripted." However, in light of the new theory, crossover experiences can be neatly explained.

When a person attunes to what someone else is actively scripting, telepathy results. When a person accesses memories scripted from previous generations, a "past life memory" is simulated. Apparitions, or "ghosts," are the same thing, with an unusual degree of self-awareness encoded into the script.

## PARALLEL TONALITY AND PILGRIM NAVIGATION

This has been posited for decades. However, the results of experiments were inconclusive, and moreover, were unsupported and ridiculed by the scientific community. Karenne Kiyakova, a graduate student of the Carpathian Protectorate University, first proved the connection between Parallel Tonality and the Pilgrim mutant ability to safely navigate dangerous areas without the benefit of maps. She posited that if they somehow knew what the previous explorers had encountered, they wouldn't *need* maps.

## PARALLEL TONALITY AND JUMP DRIVES

Jumping from point to point is dangerous. Flawless data collection, precision calculations and pinpoint maneuvering are all necessary, and there is no room for error. Faulty input from the sensors, a microfraction's divergence in result, or a less-than-exact placement of the enormous tonnage of the jump ship will result in the annihilation of everyone on board. Any delay in the jump command necessitates recalculation, and rerunning the risk of error.

*Any jump point ever used would have at least one accurate record of its precise location and drift, as well as any abnormalities which may only have been perceptible from up close. Unlike the ship's main systems, P.T. is based on a data system completely separate from the traditional sensor array, and provides accurate information despite any environmental conditions, such as extreme gravitational fluctuations.*

SCREEN 4 | query "navcom" | source=Advanced Theories of Space Navigation; 2651

## NAVCOM A.I.

2648 marked the invention of NAVCOM, an independently operating on-board computational system which is capable of reading the scripted Tonal Fields created by human minds. Currently under a great deal of controversy and highly regulated, the only currently accepted, legal, or in fact possible use of the NAVCOM is for navigational verification. Human rights questions are currently being avoided, the tacit agreement being that the preservation of human life— in light of the genocidal philosophies of the only other known space-faring race—transcends concerns of privacy.

The fields scripted around jump points are read, sifted for useful data, and checked against the ship's primary system. In practice, it works far better than predicted. So much mental concentration is devoted to the situation prior to a successful jump that the information seems "highlighted" on the resultant field. In cases of unsuccessful jumps, this phenomenon is even more striking, essentially acting as a warning beacon in dangerous territory.

NAVCOM A.I. has raised the jump success rate to nearly 100% on any previously traversed jump lines. It has a permanent data load of every known stable jump point, and a constant scan of all pertinent Tonal Fields. It dovetails with known astronomical phenomena, enabling it to accurately predict even random-seeming equipotential eclipses.

NAVCOM has removed the teeth from the monster that was space navigation. It is imperative that all Confed navigational officers understand how vital it is that this information remains the exclusive domain of mankind.

**M14TCN5 Portable Data Reader Unit**

## INQUIRY INTO THE CAPTURE AND SUBSEQUENT ESCAPE AND RETURN OF COMMANDER TAGGART

**Compiled from Debriefings, Psychological Reports & Staff Intelligence, Confederation Navy 2641.350**

### PERSONAL HISTORY

Taggart was born on Mimas Colony in 2605, genetic parents James and Bethlyn Taggart. The Taggarts perished in the initial Mimist terrorist attack of 2613. He was legally adopted by his guardian, Mikal Taggart, and his wife, Anhel Taggart, in 2614.

Due to the success of the 2624 Mimite terrorist attack—which, although famous for shutting down the colony's primary systems, also successfully deleted most of the official colonial records—there are no official records predating 2624. However, all Taggart's records post-dating that period are in order.

He attended the University of Cairo for four years, earning his level-one degree in Physical Science in 2627, graduating 23rd out of 1055.

He was admitted into Space Force OCS in 2627. Graduated with honors, subsequently attended Flight School and Counterintelligence School.

| OCS RECORD | |
|---|---|
| GPA 4.33 | Rank in Class 3 (of 221) |
| **Flight School Academic Record** | |
| GPA 4.31 | Rank in Class 20 (of 302) |
| **Flight School Flight Record** | |
| Flight 91.0 | Rank in Class 24 (of 302) |
| Marksmanship 89 | Rank in Class 22 (of 302) |
| Safety 100 (0 accidents, 0 ships lost) | Rank in Class 1 (of 302) |
| Navigation 89 | Rank in Class 28 (of 302) |

### MILITARY RECORD

First assignment to Patrol Carrier *Horus*, 2629.

Promoted to captain and transferred to Intelligence Services upon outbreak of Pilgrim hostilities. Attached to CIS for the duration of the war, record classified. Returned to flight duty 2635, with rank of Lt. Commander.

After the war, requested transfer to Exploratory Services. Promoted to Commander simultaneously with assignment to *Iason*, 2637.

Taggart is considered to be an honest, dependable officer, and an extremely competent pilot. He has never amassed many close friends, being somewhat insular in habit, but is well respected by his wingmen and fellow officers.

Taggart was apparently involved with a woman named Danielle Kura in 2627. She died of medical complications resulting from exposure to the TBM33 virus shortly before his graduation from the University of Cairo.

Taggart was listed as missing, presumed dead after the *Iason* first-contact incident. He reappeared in 2641, at Tartarus Port, and reported back to duty from a public communications booth located in the Commercial Customs section of the station.

After debriefing, he was awarded accrued pay and leave. Other than certain vitamin deficiencies and some minor parasitic infections, he was in good health. He is currently on three month's R&R leave, after which the doctors have certified him psychologically and physically ready to return to duty.

### FROM FIRST CONTACT TO THE DESTRUCTION OF THE *IASON*

*[Excerpted from 2641 debriefing]*

At 0450 hours, I was on free-time. I was in the flight sim, practicing reverse-thrust turning maneuvers, and possibly Shelton slides . . . I can't remember for certain. But I was simming when the first alarm went off. I remember I thought it was a part of the sim ship's systems, and couldn't figure which warning it was.

Then I notice that the deck lights were on Full Bright, and got out and started to run to station. It was a good battle-stations alert; everyone was in control, knew what to do. It was like a precision drill, only we knew it wasn't a drill. I don't know what we thought it was, maybe hold-out Pilgrim activity. . . .

My station was on the flight deck, of course. The three other pilots got there within a minute or two of me. The flight sim is just around the corner, so I was there in seconds. It was Hurry Up and Wait for a while.

There were only four pilots, and two Ferrets. We spent most of our time in the shuttles, ferrying the scientists around. The Ferrets had stripped-down armament and hyped-up sensors . . . really flying cameras more than anything else. Solar patrols are fully loaded with escort fighters, but not the explorers . . . of course, they had no way of knowing we'd meet anything alive out there that wasn't single-celled and growing on a rock.

. . . the captain was good about keeping us informed about events. Every fifteen minutes we'd get an info-byte about what was happening. After about an hour, Farrah Izmuti and I were ordered out. If the Ferrets had been sent out when it first happened, I'd have still been off-duty, but I went on the clock at 0700, and we went out at 0715. We were laughing at the guys who had just clocked out. . . .

Aria—that was Captain Izmuti's callsign, Aria—was ordered to make flybys of the aliens, and I was sent out to scan the area. I was flash-beaming the info back to the *Iason*, starting off with the ships themselves, and then turning the scan outwards. I was looking for anything unusual, but specifically anything that resembled another alien ship.

. . . the scans were unusual. I'd never seen anything that was alien and complex. I had experience scanning for life on planets, and I'd scanned probably two hundred Terran ships, and it was different. It was obviously alien, with completely different patterns on the scope than a human ship would put out.

I kept an eye on our backs, but started pulling the scanners in for another round of medium-range scans. That's when they fired on Aria. It was the first hostile action, and at first I thought it might have been a warning shot. She was buzzing them pretty close, and they didn't vaporize her, they just knocked her around a little. The captain ordered her back in, and she made it okay. I stayed out and kept scanning, as originally ordered.

I kept up medium- and long-range scans for close to an hour. There was a weird pulse from the alien ships, which I think was their shields readjusting in preparation for the assault, or perhaps their energy weapons coming on line. They commenced their attack on the *Iason*, and there was return fire. I had received no further orders, and although I considered making a pass on the aliens, I stayed in place, hoping that they would retreat, and I'd be able to catch the gate's fingerprint.

When the *Iason* was destroyed, I was hit by a piece of the debris. It came right at me, like someone had taken aim and fired a part of the ship directly toward me. I'm not sure exactly what part of the *Iason* it was—I was partly dazzle-blinded by the firefight, and partly . . . well, in space, looking out of the canopy doesn't usually show you much unless you've got a sun over your shoulder. It just looked like a piece of blackness, unfolding right in front of me. I didn't even know what it was. . . .

### CAPTURE AND FIRST IMPRESSIONS

Impact didn't destroy my Ferret, but it completely drained my shields and damaged my repair array. The first thing I did when I saw that the *Iason* had been destroyed was hit the self-destruct. You know, it wasn't that difficult a decision. I always expected it would be hard to make myself do it, but it seemed like a really good idea. I slapped it like a bug, and when it didn't work, I hit it again. I really got angry that it was ignoring me. That's when I noticed that all systems were down. Totally down. The only thing I can think is that some shrapnel must have punched through my shields, past my armor, and actually opened both of my power supplies.

. . . it didn't get cold as quickly as I thought it would. . . .

**M14TCN5 Portable Data Reader Unit**

I was getting punchy when I felt them pull me in. I still thought I would asphyxiate, but they cracked the canopy open before I actually passed out. When that green fog they've got started swirling around, I was sure I was going to asphyxiate, but I didn't. I didn't even pass out at first.

In fact, right off, it makes you feel pretty good. Then it makes you feel *too* good—like you're accelerating without moving—and then you pass out. I came to and passed out probably three times before I finally woke up in a filtered room.

In retrospect, I understand more things now than I did originally. For instance, the first time I woke up they were fighting, like kids fighting over a doll. One of these huge creatures was holding me under one arm, and another one would attack, and when I was dropped, another one would grab me, and then the others would attack, and so on. I got pretty cut up on each pass. . . . I think it was the pain that made me come to, really. Anyway, my brain was pretty muzzy, and I was thinking that there were good guys and bad guys fighting over me, and I was hoping the good guys won. Turns out there weren't any good guys. They just wanted me as a battle trophy, and the losers would only get to keep pieces of the Ferret.

The next thing I remember, I was on the floor, and it seemed like there was a lake of blood around me, and those guys were really fighting each other for keeps. I remember that I tried to crawl away, so I wasn't too bad off . . . then somebody fell on me, and the next time I woke up, I could see my arm had broken—the bone was sticking about an inch out of my upper arm—and I was having even more trouble breathing. . . . I think a couple of ribs had cracked.

Anyway. The next time I woke up, I was in a small room, like a storage unit or walk-in closet. On the floor in the corner was a machine. There wasn't any light, really, but it felt like someone had taken two devices, cut them in half, and silver-taped the pieces together, sideways. I'm pretty sure it was filtering the air: I didn't get that rushing feeling. I was kind of mad about that, because the pain was really bad and I was sick on top of that. Oh yes, I don't really recommend throwing up with broken ribs. . . .

Eventually, the winner came in with another, smaller alien. They were both wearing helmets that covered their faces, but I could see by the overall shape that they weren't really humanoid. For one thing, I saw fangs. My arm had stopped hurting by that point, but the smaller one started pulling on it, trying to reset the bone—they were enough like us to know how to do that, anyway—and I passed out again. We'll just skip over all the screaming . . . anyway, I know the first alien was the winner because the next time I come to, he's holding me by the throat, and it feels like he's ripping my neck into shreds. Turns out, he's scratching his name into my neck with his claw.

I don't know how long I stayed in that closet. I've been wondering if I should have tried to get out. I didn't try. I thought about it, but you know, I just didn't.

I was in there for maybe a month. I say that because my arm was pretty much healed. It was dark in there nearly all the time. There was no light in there at all. I think I got fed about once a day. I sure didn't starve. I got lots of meat and a fair amount of leafy vegetables. It was steak and spinach every day, only it wasn't steak and it wasn't spinach. I would have killed for bread.

Like I said, I was in there for several weeks, and then this pack of aliens come in, grab me and the machine in the corner, and carry me out into the hall. That's all I remember of the first ship.

## TRANSPORT AND ACCLIMATIZATION

As far as I can tell, the war was beginning to first heat up, and the commanders wanted some first-hand knowledge of who they were up against. I can't be certain. Maybe that alien . . . that Kilrathi . . . who won me in that fight had gotten in trouble, and they confiscated all of his things. There was simply no way of telling from my perspective.

I'd like to say I picked up some of their language, but I never really understood anything they said, besides the basics like "yes" and "no," and even that I couldn't pronounce myself. I did get to be pretty good at deciphering their insignia, but it didn't really make any difference. It was just a game I played to keep my mind occupied.

But I eventually woke up in a real cell, thick glass on all four sides, with the bottom three inches of the walls being open and barred, and a barred ceiling. It was an enormous room, filled entirely with row after

## SCREEN 4 | query "escape, taggart" | source=Confederation Navy Intelligence reports | 2641.350

row of glass cells. The light was dim, but at least there was enough light to see by. You have no idea how important that was. That first day, I was the only person in the entire room. It probably held thousands of humans eventually. It was hard to count—there was light, but it was still pretty dark.

At first, they kept me pretty busy. They tried all sorts of endurance tests, but I was lucky because at first I was the only one they had, so they were going out of their way to keep me alive. They did things that I had trouble trying to foil, such as how much heat or cold I could endure, things like that. I really don't remember that much about them because so many of them ended up with me passed out cold. There were times I'd wake up, and I'd have a new abrasion or whatever, and no idea how I got it. It wasn't terrible, though. It was just really, really unpleasant. I tried to screw up the results when I could, but that wasn't often.

After a while, they started bringing in more humans, and once they had a surplus, they weren't so careful. They were getting humans by the thousands, as the war started to swing back and forth. They'd take a colony, restock the cells, and as far as I could tell, kill everyone else. I was able to get updates from the few people I could talk to, the ones who could speak Standard.

Really, after they got a surplus, they didn't bother me that much anymore. It was like having a window to hell. Believe me when I tell you that they know exactly what can kill a human. Exactly.

I'm not sure, but I think I was still that first Kilrathi warrior's trophy. That's the only thing I can imagine, that would have made them leave me alone like that.

I know now that I was in there for about two years.

I have only one guess why they came and took me away. It's the trophy thing again. They came, strapped a filter device to my back and fitted a mask over my face, and took me to a launch bay. I was stuffed into something that looked like a cross between a fighter and a shuttle, and strapped into the back seat. I can only guess that I was being "returned" to the warrior that claimed me originally. I didn't particularly want to be returned, and started to work at the straps, very quietly.

We jumped about three times. The final jump landed us next to a big cruiser-type ship that was trying to laser a fast little cargo-scout. Like trying to kill a grasshopper with a cannon. Still, it was going to win, because the second that scout stopped maneuvering, or ran out of power, it would be an unarmored, unshielded target. I didn't know that when we jumped in, though. I just decided that it was now or never, got clear of the straps, and used the filter device that I was hooked up to as a club to cave in that Kilrathi pilot's skull. Kilrathi have very thick skulls. It was messy.

I didn't know how to work the controls, but I could aim the thing, so I aimed it at what I thought was the bridge. Remember I mentioned how I didn't hesitate to hit the self-destruct button on the Ferret? Same thing. Crashing that little ship into the bridge of the cruiser seemed like the best idea in the world. As it turned out, it wasn't the bridge. I don't know what it was, but it wasn't the bridge. I think it may have been an external shield generator, because I skipped off the field once, then slammed into the hull—which was unexpected—and then went spinning off into space.

. . . and I didn't pass out . . .

### RETURN TO CONFED SPACE

Next thing I know, I'm being tractored in by the Confed cargo-scout. No, I didn't believe it either. Turns out, it's a scout for . . . salvagers? . . . small, space-faring entrepreneurs? . . . really, it was part of a small band of out-of-luck pilots who buy cast-off ships, fix them up with grapples and tractors and so on, and do whatever they can to make a living. Mostly, they scavenge debris for valuable scrap. In this case, they scavenged me. Or rather, the battered and broken Kilrathi ship. I would like to formally thank the Confed for putting a bounty on any Kilrathi artifacts. . . .

Still, those marvelous gentlemen aren't exactly welcomed by the authorities, and although they sympathized with my plight, and gave me a truly memorable meal, the best they could do for me was to drop me off at a convenient port. Which they did.

That's when I reported back for duty.

**M14TCN5 Portable Data Reader Unit**

# CAPTAIN JAMES TAGGART

"The Diligent" Long- and Short-Haul Transit

### FREE TRADER
U-Web Diligent/Taggart

Passenger Charters. Bonded.

** Personal and Confidential **

TO: Admiral Tolwyn, The Concordia

Terra, 2654.056

**Geoff,**

How do you like the new letterhead? I'm greatly looking forward to beginning my adventures as a Free Trader. I expect this will be the last status report you receive directly from me, since once I'm in Vega these channels will no longer be secure. The Diligent herself seems eager to be back in space (I feel a great affinity for the old girl, and am quite sure she has a personality). The last of the special equipment arrived safely and should be installed in a day or two.

I do appreciate the amount of freedom you've given me on this assignment. I trust you'll not find it misplaced. I want to take a few moments to set out the priorities of my rather unusual commission, as I see them.

Basically, the Diligent and I will be doing pretty much what the Ebenezer and I did during the Pilgrim affair, the difference being that this time around I don't have to pretend to be anybody other than who I am . . . a broken down old spacehand trying to survive long enough to earn a comfortable retirement. I'm certainly not going to miss the prayer meetings and con/crit sessions of my former assignment (although I did rather enjoy the transcendence dances).

At the moment, I see three distinct priorities to my operations (once I get my cover firmly established, and putting aside those unique situations which I'm sure will arise).

The first and simplest of my jobs is more or less ragpicking. By that I mean finding the various hardware that the Kilrathi may have managed to stash around Vega, and either dealing with it myself or turning it over to the attention of the proper agencies. This is almost purely mechanical, but I confess a certain enthusiasm for the job.

# CAPTAIN JAMES TAGGART

"The Diligent" Long- and Short-Haul Transit

## FREE TRADER
**U-Web Diligent/Taggart**

Passenger Charters. Bonded.

There's a healthy dose of terrier to my personality, and I expect that sniffing out and digging up these Kilrathi "bones" will be a satisfying pastime. The other agreeable thing about this part of the mission is that it is best accomplished in glorious solitude.

The second priority will require getting my hands a bit dirtier. I refer to the process of ferreting out those humans who may be engaged with the Kilrathi. While seeking out and shutting down espionage proper must, of course, always remain a priority—and I'll certainly keep my eye out for it—I suspect that the thrust of my personal efforts will lie somewhat elsewhere. I'm most interested in finding those commercial outlets to the Empire. The cats may want all humanity dead and roasted in the long run, but until that day Confed has things that the cats want (and vice versa, of course). Where the desire exists, the means emerge, and if we can find our end of the Human-Kilrathi black market—however small and desperate it may be—that will be an important breakthrough. You see, when you catch a spy—especially a good one—the only thing you can really do with him is kill him. A smuggler or pirate, on the other hand, is a resource that can be used by our side (do I teach grandma how to suck eggs?). I hope to uncover such resources.

Finally, we have the Pilgrim question to consider. I must confess that when you first mentioned Pilgrim subversion, I was inclined to regard the suspicion as alarmist jingoism. Lately, however, I've been revising my opinions. I still don't see the remnants of the Alliance proper as a direct threat—our watch is too close, but more importantly they're spiritually broken. However, as Milton knew, it is not possible to kill an idea. McDaniel's words are still out there, and I would not be surprised if they find listeners in the near future. There's the colonists, of course—tension between the outer systems and Terra is growing every day. I also suggest, sir, that you look to your own officers. I do not say this to spread dissension, nor out of any disrespect for your command, but from an objective sense of history. The seductive elitism of the Pilgrim way is particularly tempting to a certain kind of military man. Sed quis custodiet ipsos custodes? If the Pilgrim ideals can find fertile ground among a force as vital as either the colonies or the military, then even the ashes of the original Alliance may start to stir.

**M14TCN5 Portable Data Reader Unit**

# CAPTAIN JAMES TAGGART

"The Diligent" Long- and Short-Haul Transit

### FREE TRADER
**U-Web Diligent/Taggart**

Passenger Charters. Bonded.

But I'll leave you to look after your staff; I'll be operating on a rather more basic level. I believe I can say without immodesty that I'm as qualified as anyone you've got to look for manifestations of Pilgrim thought, however they may emerge. Nouveau-Pilgrims may try to take advantage of the Kilrathi crisis for their own ends (insanity, of course, but we are speaking of fanatics here), and the possibility of Pilgrim-Kilrathi alliance cannot be discounted. The Nazis and the Japanese had no trouble finding one another.

I trust that the above priorities meet with your approval, and again my thanks for this chance to be of service to Confed and Humanity.

My best to Gillian and the rest of the crew at the spookhouse.

Warmest regards,

*Jim Taggart*

P.S. Just got the names of my outbound supercargo. Knowing you, I'm sure it's safe to presume that it's no coincidence that the son of Arnold Blair (or, more particularly, the son of Devi Soulsong) has been assigned to my ship. I knew Devi quite well, and I knew her grandfather, old Solomon Truepath, as well. I imagine you're keeping a weather-eye on young Lieutenant Blair. If the Truepath heritage continues in the Blair boy . . . well, I'm sure we both understand the significance.

I'll certainly give this Blair a good once-over, although I must confess I hope there's nothing amiss with the lad . . . his parents deserved so much better than they got. I've always applauded your decision to allow them to rest in peace. But I tarry too long among old ghosts.